Mercury Is Hot

Steve Rzasa

Mercury Is Hot by Steve Rzasa
www.steverzasa.com

INTERSTICE BOOKS and the INTERSTICE BOOKS logo are trademarks of Steve Rzasa. Absence of TM in connection with marks of Interstice or other parties does not indicate an absence of trademark protection of those marks.

This is a work of fiction. Names, characters, places, and incidents are products of the author's imagination or are used fictitiously. Any similarity to actual people, organizations, and/or events is purely coincidental.

Cover illustration: Tithi Luadthong
Layout and design: Steve Rzasa

International Standard Book Number: 9781733585163

Books

Urban Fantasy
> *Mercury On Guard*
> *Mercury For Hire*
> *Mercury At Risk*
> *Mercury Is Hot*

Space Opera
> *The Word Reclaimed: The Face of the Deep 1.0*
> *The Word Unleashed: The Face of the Deep 2.0*
> *Broken Sight: The Face of the Deep 2.5*
> *The Word Endangered: The Face of the Deep 3.0*
> *Severed Signals*
> *Cryptic Commands*
> *Failed Frequencies*
> *Mixed Messages*
> *Empire's Rift: A Takamo Universe Novel*
> *Strife's Cost: A Takamo Universe Novel*

Science-Fiction
> *Man Behind the Wheel*
> *Multiverse*
> *For Us Humans*
> *The Echo Watch*

Superhero
> *Airfoil: Origins*

Fantasy
> *The Bloodheart*
> *The Lightningfall*
> *Just Dumb Enough (contributor & editor)*

Steampunk
> *Crosswind: The First Sark Brothers Tale*
> *Sandstorm: The Second Sark Brothers Tale*

CHAPTER ONE

October

I was wrapping my brain around the difference between a red blend and a merlot—and why I should care—when the ten-foot-wide flaming meatball burned a path down the hillside.

Had to figure. It was the first gorgeous day we'd had after two weeks of gloom. Everything was still brittle and dry, because as much as the clouds had threatened, we hadn't gotten a drop of rain. With zero clouds and a sky so blue it bordered on fake, everyone was out and about in short sleeves and, well, shorts. Royal's Roadside was the perfect place to spend the afternoon. Where else could you buy locally made cheeses, farm-fresh produce, and a bottle of wine for a certain fiancée who wanted to spend a romantic evening together?

Sounded like a great way to end the day before the giant whatever it was interrupted.

It broke through the tree line, hit the ditch, and catapulted across the 311. Good thing traffic through the Arbor Valley was light or it would have pulverized a car—which it wound up doing when it slammed into a row of parked vehicles on the opposite side. Bashed into a tiny Corolla sandwich between two Dodge Rams, scorching the paint on both pickups. The Corolla crumpled, permanently reshaped into a huge metal catcher's mitt.

I felt for the owner of the car. Seriously. But I was also super happy it wasn't my ride.

People shouted and screamed. They dropped bags. Tomatoes spattered on the pavement. It was a mad scramble for car keys and dash for driver's side doors. Me? I slapped two twenties down on the counter, said, "Keep the change," and sprinted across the road.

"Sprinted" is an exaggeration. It was more a speedy limp. Such is the case when you've had to cut off one of your legs in the course of saving the world. But, hey, the world wasn't destroyed, and I got a robotic prosthetic. And it was sunny.

Either way, I wouldn't be much help cleaning up wrecked cars, but since the giant flameball sprouted tentacles, I knew my expertise was required.

There was no mistaking the shriek of an astral fiend.

I was used to hearing it echo among buildings in downtown San Camillo or banging off the sides of an abandoned warehouse. Was not expecting it to set the junipers lining the highway on fire and every bird within a hundred yards flapping for safety, the dumb ones that hadn't already fled, that is.

"Hey!" Fred Royal, the farm stand owner, waved his phone. "You best stay back, son! Cops and fire are coming!"

"Thanks for the heads up!" I pulled the pulsar stave from under my shirt. I never went anywhere without the foot-long staff made of ice-cold metal. A quick twist sent golden-white light rippling through the swirling patterns etched into its sides. "I got this."

He frowned with the exact same expression of my foster dads' whenever I bluffed my way through being late for curfew. Tried to bluff, that is.

I bet his skepticism vanished when the astral fiend on fire flung the crushed door off the Corolla at me and I used a streamer of energy from the pulsar stave to slice it in half as I ran. Didn't even break a sweat.

So, this was new. Astral fiends don't catch on fire. Gaping maw full of fangs? Check. Covered in a glistening black hide? Yep. Hideous red eyes that gave you nightmares? Absolutely.

This guy looked as dry as the proverbial bone. No slime. No blue ooze. The flames distorted his features, giving him a much lighter appearance, like a coal left too long in the campfire. He speared the rest of the wrecked car and flipped it overhead. It crashed among the trees, away from people, which was great, except it meant stands of junipers on *both* sides of the highway were burning. Didn't bode well for Royal's.

I slapped at my earbud a bit too hard. Felt like it'd been punched. Note to self: Don't try that again while running. "Hey, Liz! If no one's gotten ahold of the fire department, you'd better get them here ASAP."

"Fire? What kind of fire?" She sounded excited and terrified and there could have been a squeaking sound like her chair bouncing from inside Procyon Foundation's temporary Tracking office. "The tachyon spike I registered is out of phase with the normal readings we get for a rip and I didn't think it was a big deal because we get weird stuff all the time so when it showed up in the daylight instead of late at night—"

"Liz! Fire! The burning kind!" I leapt atop the hood of one of the two damaged pickups, vaulted off, and slashed through the nearest tentacle. It flopped to the ground, writhing and steaming. Blue ooze splattered me, the truck, and the screaming teen for whom it'd been reaching. No way I was going to let anyone become a freeze-dried mummy because this astral fiend had gotten the munchies and was keen on draining life from any human within reach.

That got Roasty's attention. He went from cornering an older couple to facing me, a gaping mouth filled with jagged fangs suddenly less than six feet from my face. I pivoted midair, twisting to make an Olympic gymnast proud. Tentacles came at me from every which way.

You'd think I'd get used to the fiends' tendency to invert themselves at will, but no, it surprised me every time. Of course, they liked to switch up their tactics, and apparently had added catching on fire to their repertoire.

Right about then was when my leg seized up. It wouldn't bend when it was supposed to, which meant that instead of sticking an incredible superhero landing, I crunched onto the gravel shoulder of the road, knee first.

"Drone Eight's on its way!" Liz said. "I'll have visual soon. Police and fire are incoming, so you'd better have it cleaned up before they get there."

The astral fiend—fireball?—wasn't the brightest of creatures to breach the wall between the Interstice and this dimension, but it wasn't a chump, either. Roasty slapped at me with two spike-sheathed tentacles, the appendages made even more unpleasant by the heat shimmering off them.

But I broke the pulsar stave into its twin halves and formed and X over my head. The tentacles crashed down. The resulting explosion blew out four sets of truck windows, sending bits of molten glass skyward like reverse rain.

Again, super glad none of that was happening to my ride.

"Sure thing, Liz!" I said through gritted teeth. "No prob!"

The weight shoved me toward the ground. The fiend's shriek pummeled my head. Come on, man. I had a date tonight!

"Oh, good! Want me to send Wilhelmina for backup?"

"No way!" My seventy-something mentor? If

she saved my butt, I'd never live it down. I shoved back, with a guttural cry that wasn't anywhere as intimidating as the monster's and got enough room between us I could roll free. Or sort of stagger, I guess. *Come on, gimpy, move it!* Didn't really think my prosthetic leg would respond to insults, but I needed to regain full mobility. Preferably before I died.

It finally responded the way I wanted, as in, like a real-live leg. Didn't banish the pain shooting through what remained above the knee. Nothing ever did. But it got me to about 90 percent of my slick moves.

I slashed through an onrushing tentacle and drew on the stave's energy until I felt like I was jittery from drinking every last drop of coffee at The Shattered Mug.

Then I somersaulted right over the fiend's lumpy mass.

"You'd better move faster!" Liz yelped. "There's a surge in tachyon emissions consistent with regeneration, you know, like when an astral fiend subsumes an injured monster and doubles in size."

"Fun stuff." I skidded between smoldering junipers, creating a dust cloud that obscured my location yet, shockingly enough, didn't taste great. I spat grit from between my teeth. "Hey, if you're having a blast tracking my movements from Drone Eight, how's about you take a break and run a diagnostic on Leg 2.1? It froze up again."

"Oh, sorry. Was it the capacitor? It should be holding onto the charge from the pulsar stave whenever you—"

The rest of her Mississippi River-length sentence drowned under the thunder crack of the nearest tree shattering. Roasty found me. And Liz was right: He'd grown back one of the three tentacles I'd snipped. Which was, yeah, bad.

I ran, which as advertised before, was more off-balance than I'd have liked. Still hadn't gotten back to the normal gait, not even with a high-tech artificial leg powered by the same extra-dimensional energies that fueled the pulsar stave.

"—And if it hadn't recovered, I'd be ready for the next version." How Liz kept talking without coming up for air, I hadn't a clue. "Hey, are you okay?"

"Nope! Not okay! Where's police and fire?" Trees were torches around me. Those gentle breezes that lent relief from the blazing sun overhead aided the spread of the flames. And even though most people had fled the scene, it was far from safe.

Fred Royal wielded a fire extinguisher against the fire licking at the edges of his farm stand plot like he was holding back insurgents in Afghanistan. His efforts didn't prevent a long wooden shelf of assorted fruits from burning up. His shouts brought a couple teen boys running down the dirt road that wound between the trees behind the stand. One of them unfurled a hose from a shed and sprayed water as best he could.

Okay, so burnt fruit wasn't as high on the list of emergencies for a lot of people as, say, the ripping of space-time between our sunny dimension and the dark, dismal Interstice from which the astral fiends hailed. But I couldn't watch this idiot monster's flailing destroy the livelihood of a guy like Fred.

"Hey!" I smacked the pulsar staves off a pair of trees. The fiery fiend bellowed in my face. "Don't forget the main course!"

It screamed and charged me.

I returned the favor.

There were no fancy acrobatics, no risking a malfunction of my wonky leg. I gave the beast exactly what it wanted—me, thrown into its grasping tentacles. They lashed the air around me, slicing through my shirt, opening a cut here and a slash there on my skin, but the stave had a bonus that it granted besides better reflexes and minor superpowers. I could heal faster than the average Joe, which probably had something to do with me not being a native American.

Being born in another dimension had its advantages.

I cut Roasty down from eight tentacles to seven, six, five, my weapons a blur so that I didn't give him any time in which to regenerate. The downside? I got hurt more. And it put me way too close. Closer than I liked.

Close enough for him to finally wrap a spiky appendage around my neck.

Imagine taking a "polar bear" plunge. You know, the one that crazy folks who live in a state that actually has winter take by jumping into the iciest water imaginable. Except this ice permeated my skin, flowed through my veins, and hammered at my heart.

I gasped.

Couldn't see straight. Heck, everything was sliding into gray. Liz shouted into my ear. Sirens wailed nearby—or way off? Nothing made sense. I wanted the pain to end. Fingers scrabbled at the weight pressing on my throat. Whatever energies the pulsar stave granted me drained away, leaving me with as much fighting strength as a teenager who'd been stuck in bed with the flu for a week.

Then my fake leg went dead.

Of course it did. Because it used the power I absorbed from the pulsar stave.

Mercury…

Great. The voice was back.

You're never out of our reach. We're always on the other side of the wall. Listening, Whispering.

I gritted my teeth. One half of the pulsar stave was on the ground. The other? Still clutched in one hand, bleeding just enough power to keep me from being drained to death by the fiend—and, apparently, keeping his flaming hide from burning me, because even though I felt like I was standing way too close to an open oven, I wasn't in need of hospitalization yet.

Mercury…

No way. Marigold Yen and Alexander Arkwright and the Whisperer could take their collective haunting voices and shove them.

"Mercury!"

Gunfire blew through the fog clogging my hearing. Sounds returned to normal as bullets shredded the fiend's face. And as if that weren't enough, water engulfed us. Weird. Not a cloud in the sky, like I'd said. But we got drenched all the same. The fiend howled so loud I thought my eardrums would burst. Then, it dropped me.

Finally.

Life, riding along the wave front of the pulsar staves' energy, surged through my body. I was manic with power. I slammed the halves back together and swung with all my might.

Roasty vanished in a burst of purple light that felled a dozen trees and sent me tumbling end over end.

That's where I was when Lt. Gabriel Ramos, San Camillo Police Department, found me—upside down, against a trunk, my face mashed into a muddy shrub.

"Hang on. EMTs are on the way." Ramos knelt beside me. He reeked of cordite. The smell was undercut by aftershave. The guy was dressed like he'd stepped out of the nearest pew, in a coral shirt lacking the smallest wrinkles, rose-colored tie secured with a silver cross for a tie-tack, and khakis ironed so sharply he could cut down the nearest trees. I could see myself inverted on his shined shoes. "But you got it, didn't you?"

"Nope. Sorry." I spit dirt, again. Twice in one fight was too many times. I pulled myself upright. "Plus, I left my supersuit at home."

Ramos smirked. He tilted mirrored sunglasses up. "The filth smeared all over your face did a good job keeping your identity safe. Not that you've ever been particularly concerned about that aspect of your heroism."

I rolled my eyes at that word. "Heroism," not "aspect." "What about the fires?"

Ramos helped me upright and offered himself as a human crutch as I staggered back to the road. My leg was up and running, for the moment. "This portion's knocked down. FD is working across the road."

They'd hosed down the farm stand pretty good, it seemed, because nothing over there was burning. Looked like Royal's lost just the one rack, though they had a lot of produce that got extra washed.

No sign of the fiend, though.

"What was that thing?" Ramos asked.

"Astral fiend." I wiped mud from my eyes.

"Are you sure?"

"Well, it tried to suck my life out using ice-cold tentacles and tended to scream a lot, so, yes."

Ramos glowered, that oh-so-familiar angry dad combined with disapproving teacher look. "I meant, because it was dripping flames everywhere."

"Yeah. Not normal." I coughed. Smoke or water? Take your pick. I tried for the earbud—gently, this time. "Liz? Still there?"

"Yes, and you'd better explain why you went dead on your comms—"

"Lay off, will you? Roasty got away."

"Roasty?"

"The fiend. The one on fire. Flaming meatball." I shook my head, hoping Drone Eight was nearby getting footage of my exasperation. "Teleported. So, if you got any insights from the tachyon readouts, the sooner we go over the data, the better."

"Yeah, I know, I know." Liz switched over to an exaggerated whisper. "I meant, you know, Ms. Lark is *right here* and..."

She left the rest unsaid. I grimaced. "Hey, Loredana. Weren't you downtown shopping? Didn't think you'd be in the office."

"Plans change, especially when one's fiancé has found himself embroiled in a dimensional incursion of a unique nature." I couldn't help grinning at the cool, collected British tones filtering through the earbud. "Perhaps we should discuss it in detail when you return."

"How about in private?"

You can hear people smile. I can guarantee it. "If that's more to your liking."

"Definitely to my liking."

Ramos sighed. "The sooner you two get married, the better."

I winked at him. "Let's go find my car so I can blow this farm stand."

"Mercury?" Loredana again. "Don't forget the wine."

Wine? I looked around. Ah. There it was, one soggy paper bag in the middle of the 311, courtesy of the smashed bottle of red blend inside. The cheeses were flatter than, well, the paper bag.

"Yeah," I said. "About that..."

CHAPTER TWO

I hung a right at the site of our destroyed base before heading north to Procyon's new secret headquarters.

Don't ask me whether it was a good idea to route their employees' commute past their former waterfront location. I bet the foundation's psychologist had her schedule full dealing with the aftermath of last month. You know, the part where an evil, sentient ancient relic tried to drown San Camillo under a deluge made from the city's own bay? And that was after my nemesis, Alexander Arkwright, used a very selective earthquake powered by that relic to level Procyon's three towers.

I gripped the steering wheel tighter as I drove the Subaru up Bay Avenue. All the rubble was gone. Bulldozers had flattened the lot. They'd even ripped up the parking lot. Only the stone sign by the guard post remained, a silver star flanked by black parallelograms. Sure, Procyon's architect was busy on designs and would have something new in the works soon, and all the civilian employees were relocated to rented offices a few blocks away.

That didn't make it any easier to see.

I said "civilian" because most of Procyon's workers were the office types who handled the foundation's public face. They filed grant applications for housing projects and community resource centers. They fielded calls about improving run-down neighborhoods. All such things got routed up the chain of command to Loredana Lark and the manager, Hector Alvarez.

But those two had bigger things on their minds.

Procyon's real reason for existence was to safeguard our dimension from encroachment by astral fiends, like the fiery version I'd just chased off. How? By getting people like me to slay those monsters with the pulsar stave, the weapon that only individuals with certain genetic markers could use.

Recent catastrophes had opened the eyes of the general public, though. The internet was full of whispers. Not the kind that bugged me in the middle of the night. Those were nightmares brought on by the unholy aberration that combined Marigold Yen—a former friend—and Arkwright with the nebulous Whisperer. What they were up to inside the Interstice was anybody's guess, but if you guessed "bad stuff," you'd win a prize.

Seemed like the "bad stuff" now included new and customized astral fiends.

I drove out the north side of town, up the coast

along the 311. Waves crashed along the seaside rocks. An old monastery peeked over the cliffs to my right, a distant sentinel.

The next turn onto a side road led into a hilly backcountry filled with scrub pines. I used the word road loosely because it was more a rutted path meant for horses and mountain bikes. The Subaru bounced over rocks. Branches brushed at the side mirrors.

Ramos grimaced. He braced his hand against the ceiling. "I'd have refused the ride if I'd know the condition of the road was so poor."

"Quit whining. There's no sense having a secret base if you're gonna have the path to it paved smooth." We jounced around a corner. Okay, it was rough, even for my preferences. But thankfully, it flattened out a hundred yards down the twisting, winding track into a passable dirt road that showed signs of recent improvement. The trees were taller here, reaching out far enough to shade the road from most of the sun—and snooping satellites.

Ramos checked his phone. "Bradley says they've got the scene cleaned up."

"How is Detective Surly these days?"

"You know Stan. I thought the vein on his forehead would burst when I told him I was riding with you instead of heading back to the precinct. But he can't complain too much, seeing as how partnering with me on the new task force means he has a degree of autonomy he never enjoyed working Homicide."

"Sounds good to me, as long as Homicide and

the rest of SCPD—task force included—doesn't know where Procyon hides its fun stuff these days." I caught a glimpse of weather-beaten concrete through the trees. "Garage is coming up."

"Don't worry, I'm keeping it classified." Ramos craned his neck. "When you say garage, you mean… What is that?"

"That, my friend, is an off-the-books, repurposed Titan-II ballistic missile launch site." Turned out that the superhero Airfoil way out East in Drake City wasn't the only one who liked the idea of using an abandoned military base for his lair—unless lair is the word only bad guys use. Never mind.

The garage in question was a low, slanted concrete bunker that someone had cut a brand-new entrance into. Four flat pads, these also crumbling concrete, spread across the clearing. Scrub pines had grown up in between them during the intervening decades.

A steel door trundled open, descending into the floor. I drove us down a shallow ramp, dimly lit with soft amber lights, as the door sealed us in. The ramp curved, following the sides of what had been the main silo, except Procyon's enterprising souls had a parking garage built into the mid-level. I tucked the Subaru between a pair of Procyon Security SUVs, their silver flanks reflecting orange. I spotted Loredana's glitzy BMW a couple spots down.

The car door made a tremendous echo in the cavernous space. Ramos peered over the railing. "I'll admit, I'm impressed."

"Awesome, right?" I led him to a door and flashed my Procyon ID badge. The panel to the right blinked from red to green. "A regular Batcave."

"Don't even tell me Procyon put this together since the Hedron quake."

The name of the sentient artifact that had tried to annihilate San Camillo—Hedron of Orbits—still made me shudder. "Nah. It's been a backup for forty years. Kept in mothballs, but periodically updated with tech. Liz has been—well, check it out."

There was a security cubicle of glass and steel just inside the door. Garvey had his feet up on the desk. Dude was the size of a small mountain, so it was a wonder the desk didn't collapse. Muscles protested their confinement inside a black polo shirt emblazoned with the Procyon star logo. He glanced up from a bank of monitors, each one showing a different aspect of the exterior, the silo and its garage, and other compartments. "Mr. Hale. Ms. Lark said you'd be bringing a guest."

Ramos offered his badge and credentials.

"Thanks, Lieutenant. You're cleared." Garvey nodded.

I tossed him a mock salute and led us down the metal tube that served as one of the connecting corridors. The curved walls were painted a soft white. Recessed lighting gave it a bright, warm feeling. Whatever they used for floor tiling muted our footsteps.

"Homey," Ramos said.

I shrugged. "I'd rather have the views of San Camillo Bay again, but it's nice to stay unbothered. And you know, since we've been out in public a bunch lately, we need a little more privacy."

"You really should carry your suit on you for such emergencies as the one we just had."

"Seriously? I can't fit it inside a ring, Ramos, and don't even think about suggesting a man-purse."

"What about Airfoil? He has to have some way to store his suit."

"We haven't talked about it."

"That doesn't make any sense." Ramos frowned. "He's been far more used to performing in the public eye than you, Mercury. Seems like the perfect person from whom you could take tips."

I rolled my eyes. "Fine. I'll hit him up on Instagram and we can share disguise pics."

Ramos muttered something that sounded like *estupido* but I pretended like I didn't care. Because I didn't, really.

We made a sharp turn and faced a door of green metal. The word "Tracking" was stenciled in white. My ID granted us access yet again.

Really, Liz had made sure it felt just like the old Tracking. There was little lighting, save what came from dozens of computer monitors and three huge screens at the front of the room. Desks were arranged in a semi-circle, with Liz's console in the center. Very Star Trek.

Bright red Converse sneakers kicked together to the tinny sounds of reggae filtering from her computer. Those sneakers were all I could see protruding from under the desk. I nudged one with my shoe. "Boo."

She yelped. Elizabeth Stojan slid out, her eyes wide with surprise. Her scowl morphed into a grin when she saw me. "Hey, Mercury! I'm resetting the sensor parameters that we've been feeding through the drones. Cyril needed a new processor to handle the load."

Cyril. Her personal computer. Not surprising she named it, because she named lots of things, like her algorithm called the Big Bad Wolf that was handy for cracking systems it shouldn't.

She hopped back up into her seat and brushed dust from hair dyed a brilliant neon pink. "And you brought Ramos! Cool! You guys want to see what I found out?"

"The tour's been interesting, but yes, that's why I'm here." Ramos folded his arms.

"Oh. Sure." Even I could tell when Liz's Middle Eastern complexion darkened from embarrassment. "Okay, so, here's the tachyon readouts."

I squinted at the bevy of lines squiggling across the big center monitor. "The build-up to the rip looks the same as we're used to, but what's with all—those? The ones from right after?"

"I don't know." Liz rubbed her hands together. "Isn't it great? It's an entirely new curve that I can't find any reference to in our databases but of course

I don't have all our files to help me do an exhaustive search because a lot of stuff from the Historic Vault is still locked up—"

"And we have gaps in said 'stuff,' Elizabeth." Loredana Lark was the only person in Tracking who didn't look like she was a tech geek. Tall, lithe, wearing a classy navy-blue dress with short sleeves, she should have been making a presentation to the Chamber of Commerce at a late-night gala. "Lieutenant. Nice to see you."

Ramos shook her hand. "Likewise, Loredana."

"I see you brought Mercury back to me in one piece." She smiled.

"I do what I can." Ramos clapped me on the back. "I'm sure he'll tell you he had the situation well in hand."

"Which I did, by the way." I kissed Loredana. "Seriously, it wasn't that bad."

She looped her arm around my waist, a subtle gesture that drew her closer to me but didn't break her poise. "Indeed? Drone Eight shows someone who looks remarkably like you making a reckless charge at an unknown variety of astral fiend."

"Roasty," Liz said.

I pantomimed shushing her, finger to my lips.

Loredana's eyebrow arched. "Roasty? So, we're giving them colloquial classifications?"

"Look, it wasn't the ideal solution, but I was running out of ideas. My normal flip, dodge, and slice repertoire wasn't cutting it—pun intended."

"I was teasing, Mercury."

"Could have fooled me." I grinned.

Ramos cleared his throat. "Can I interrupt another awkward moment between our lovebirds to get us back to the briefing? This case just became my priority, per the task force's injunction."

"Of course." Loredana tapped her fingernails on the back of Liz's chair. "Please continue, Elizabeth."

"Sure!" She tilted the largest of the three flat screen monitors cordoning her desk, turning it into a giant tablet. A few swipes made the tachyon readouts on the big screen shrink to one side. A fuzzy magnification of the fiery astral fiend took its place. The image sprouted lines linked to—well, gibberish, from my standpoint. I mean, I did okay in Math and Science up through community college, but that stuff was what we had people like Liz for. "This guy matches up with only about 78 percent of the composition of the typical astral fiend."

"The fire wasn't a dead giveaway?" I quipped.

Loredana nudged me but she was still smiling so I counted that as a win.

"It's more than that. So, the readings from Drone Eight fed me back a bunch of weird stuff. Like, I haven't seen anything like it. I mean, it kinda reminded me of the fiend-hound, in the way its composition was mixed with that of a real canine."

Fiend-hound. Right. The hideous mingling of astral fiend and good old-fashioned mutt that escaped from the labs of Syndax Multinational when

Arkwright was experimenting in tachyon absorption. I was really hoping that didn't mean we had a zombie resurgence on our hands, either, because neither type of creature was fun to tangle with. "Can you tell what it was mingled with?"

"Not yet. But I can re-task our drones to watch for variations in tachyon flux exhibited by the rip that dropped off this fiery guy—Roasty. That may give us some lead-in time." Liz shook her head. "Too bad we don't have Forecasting anymore."

"The department isn't disbanded. It's merely—on hiatus," Loredana said.

"Because Marigold Yen was the one interpreting her dreams so she could Forecast where astral fiends would appear before they showed up, and she turned out to be part of a matrilineal conspiracy to steal Procyon's secret weapons," I added.

Ramos scowled at me.

"What? I was being helpful. Besides, Liz is right. Until Procyon restocks Forecasting, our response window is tiny. Any advantage she can give us is better than none."

"Very well. Re-task the drones, Elizabeth, and keep us apprised." Loredana checked her phone. "Can you provide us with an ETA on the creature's return? Assuming it will return."

"Oh, it should. I mean, if it works like the fiend-hound did, it might not have left our world. It's probably skipped off somewhere nearby. I'll deploy the drones around the county and see what we can call up." Liz grinned. "It'll take me a while, so, uh, if you guys have other plans—"

"Quite." Loredana clasped her hands behind her back. "If you have no questions for us, Lieutenant…"

Ramos sighed. "No, nothing that'll be of use. If Liz can send me whatever news she gets from the drones in a timely fashion, I'll get our squad out as fast as I can. Assuming Mercury needs backup."

"Mercury does." I sat on the edge of Liz's desk and stretched my leg. A sturdy press of a recessed latch unhooked the prosthetic from the stump. I exhaled, glad to be rid of it for a moment. I handed Liz the fake leg. "Can you run me a diagnostic on this? I'll take the spare."

"Sure." Liz set my souped-up leg on her desk. She reached behind a counter and pulled out a much simpler, lighter model—titanium core, custom printed shell of glossy black material speckled with stars. "Version 1.0."

"Not my favorite, but at least it didn't glitch." It was just plastic and metal. Sturdy, sure, but not supercharged. I attached it and gave it a couple of swings. "Well, next thing up is a shower, unless you've got other plans, Loredana."

"You're forgetting we have a prior engagement, thanks in no small part to your heroic actions at the farm stand."

"Oh yeah? Key to the city?"

Ramos covered his mouth. Was he laughing?

"Hardly." Loredana pursed her lips. She headed

for the door, her finger crooked, beckoning me to follow. "We have to go shopping."

"Since when?"

"Since you owe me a bottle of wine."

I smirked and hopped off the table. "Lead the way, my lady."

"At the very least," Ramos said, "You can drop me at the precinct first."

CHAPTER THREE

oredana's condo was in Tabb Terrace, the oddly terrace-less section of a nicer neighborhood of northeast San Camillo. By the time we picked up a replacement bottle of wine and assorted appetizers—and dropped Ramos at the Ninth Precinct—evening was setting in.

I sliced chunks of cheese as Loredana poured us a couple glasses of the red blend. It was bold, brilliant scarlet against the rest of her home, which was a study in how many variations of white and cream you could pack into a single living space. A warm breeze brushed aside the curtains of the open bay windows. No big surprise when my phone's weather alert squawked about the prevalent fire conditions.

"It's a miracle the hills aren't constantly alight." Loredana carried the glasses to the window and curled up in one of the corners. "Joining me?"

"Once I'm through slaving away." I flung a napkin over my arm and held a paper plate of cheese and olives above my head like I was navigating tables at the finest bistro in the city. "Dinner is served, milady."

"How lovely." Loredana handed me a glass as I set the plate between us. It'd make more sense to have the windows shut and the AC going, but the early evening weather was pleasant and dry. Not unlike the wine. "Your setback doesn't seem to have affected you."

"Setback?"

She nudged my prosthetic leg with her bare toes. "The glitch."

"Ah. That." I repositioned until I was comfortable, not an easy task when one of your limbs is devoid of all sensation. Plus, I didn't want her glancing at it all evening. Yeah, I was wearing shorts, but that didn't mean I had gotten over the inordinate amount of attention people gave my fake leg. Seriously, you'd think it had a big Post-it note that said, "Please gawk and wonder what happened to the real thing" for as many times as people stared when I was out in public. "Liz can fix it. Not like it hasn't hit a few speed bumps before. It's just, I'd rather not have it freak out when I'm face to face with another astral fiend."

"Understandably so. This new aberration: Do you think it the work of the Whisperer?"

"Really don't want to think about that. Because it wasn't bad enough when he absorbed Marigold— now he's got Arkwright rattling around with him in the Interstice. I prefer my villains one at a time, thanks very much."

Her lips twisted into that combination of amused smile and serious thought that I'd come to love. "Don't we all. In all seriousness, Mercury, tussling with astral fiends is one thing. Goodness knows Procyon has ample experience in that arena. But fiends with an altered form? This bodes of a phenomenon that, whether intentional or nature, does not bode well."

"Natural? You mean, accidental?"

"Elizabeth is contemplating a theory that has to do with merging dimensions and the unfortunate results thereof. I've set it aside until she can provide me more evidence. In the meantime, I suggest we stay on alert."

I drained half my glass.

"You are supposed to sip, darling," she said.

"Yeah, well, when you say 'alert' that usually means 'get ready to go out for a busy night trolling for monsters,' so I figured I'd accelerate my relaxing." I grinned. "Besides, it's the only way I can put up with another episode of *Dr. Who*."

Her expression didn't change but a piece of brie shot through the air and rebounded off my forehead.

We passed the rest of the evening in pleasant conversation, working on the wine—which, yes, I sipped—and relocated to the couch because she was intent on that episode, no matter how much I teased her about it. The show passed in a blur of us curled against each other, her head resting on my chest, my feet up on the coffee table. Had to admit, watching an actress portraying Agatha Christie contend with a giant evil space hornet was pretty fun, though the monster slayer aspect of my personality kept trying to critique their handling of the beast. I mean, come on, somebody slice the thing in half, already!

Somewhere amid the talking and the laughing and the wine, I dozed off as David Tennant was staring into the middle distance like he does so well.

I wish I could say it was all romantic walks on the beach. No such luck. Astral fiends hounded my every step. Tentacles dragged me into the Interstice, where dust storms scoured my skin. I collapsed. No prosthetic leg to hold me up.

You failed this time.

Him again. The Whisperer. The dark shadow that walked among the fiends. Their general and my archenemy—okay, the amalgamation of three archenemies.

What will you do when you fall again? Procyon is crippled, just like you.

I snapped free. Sweat soaked my shirt. I was gonna contend with serious body odor before too long.

Loredana was leaning on my shoulder. She didn't have to look up from the episode. "Nightmares?"

"Prize for the pretty lady." I ran a hand through my hair. "You know, I could live this life of monster-slaying with ease if I didn't have to suffer the bad dreams."

"Couldn't we all." She poked me. "I take it, then, that you missed my prior sentence."

"Probably, if I was asleep."

She poked me again. "I asked if you'd given the date any thought beyond our last conversation."

Date? Ah. *The* date. "Right. Christmas is the big day."

"Dad will gripe mightily about traveling during the holiday. The crowds at Heathrow—"

"Oh, come on. He took out corpse-fiends with a sniper rifle. Certified zombie killer, in my view. Is he really gonna let tourists and TSA keep him in England?"

"Hardly. But he'll fuss nonetheless." Loredana nodded, not at me, but at the prospect of future wedded bliss, I assumed. "Very well. Christmas it is. And the venue?"

"Working on it."

She raised an eyebrow.

"Hey, I'm working on it. Ramos suggested we tie the knot in his church."

"That sounds delightful. He's kind enough to welcome us into his home. You should value that."

I valued a world of a lot more than Ramos sharing a pew. He'd always had my back. Right now, he was probably at San Camillo's Ninth Precinct, bringing his squad up to speed on the fireball creature that had shown up. He'd be ready to face it, with just his gun and his badge and his prayers.

"Mercury?"

The TV screen was blank. Show was over. I stretched my arms. "I'd better get home. Got all that venue planning to do, you know."

"Stay for a while, won't you? We can talk about where we can have the reception if the restaurant is busy."

"What're the odds Saito-on-sky will be busy at Christmas?"

"High. Which is why I suggested you place the call two weeks ago."

"Which I did." I grinned. "And I've been bothering them weekly. So, give me a bit longer and—"

My phone buzzed. It was Liz. Which meant this relaxing interlude was going to come to an abrupt and likely dangerous ending. "Yello."

"Oh, hey, Mercury! Sorry to bother you but I thought you'd like to know we were getting some great results from the drones after I uploaded the new software that lets them monitor for tachyon flux."

"That's awesome. I'm super happy." I massaged my forehead. Really wished I was more into *Dr. Who*, so I could boot up the next episode. But Loredana was already off the couch. She poured herself a glass of water, watching me from the kitchen as she drank. "What kind of results?"

"Um… Good ones."

"Specifics, Liz."

"Oh, sure! I mean, I knew that. The coordinates are incoming to your phone. Of the astral fire-fiend,

I mean."

"Roasty's back? Where at?"

Another buzz. I lifted the phone from my face. Yep, coordinates. I put Liz on speaker and woke up my mapping app.

"What is the location?" Loredana asked.

"Out in the sticks. Not far from our first fight." I dug my car keys from my pocket and stood up. Not dizzy, so that was good. Getting a DUI on the way to vanquish a beast from another dimension would not be a great way to end the evening. "Get me visuals when you can. I'm headed out."

Loredana intercepted me at the door. "Elizabeth? Pass the word to Ms. Crown."

"Whoa, wait, I don't think we need to bug Wilhelmina with this one."

"We do and we will." Loredana folded her arms. "I'll remind you who your handler is."

"I could so make a play on words—"

"And I would be happy to hear it when the threat is neutralized. You'll have a better chance at doing so with a second warrior on your side." Loredana pursed her lips. "Especially given that your more combat-specific prosthesis is in the shop, as it were."

Translation: She didn't think I could hack the job on my plain old fake leg. "Fine. I'll go get her, since I need a chaperone."

Loredana sighed. "That isn't what I meant. I want you back safe."

"And I can't do that solo anymore, apparently."

"Mercury—"

Liz cleared her throat. Kinda forgot she was still listening in on speaker phone. "I, um, notified Wilhelmina. She's waiting for you to pick her up."

"On my way." I glanced at Loredana. "Look, I—"

"We'll discuss it later." She kissed me. "Alone or with a partner, watch yourself."

"As long as you're watching me."

"I will be in Tracking, rest assured."

Rest. I'd be happy to do that, minus nightmares. Fingers crossed that slicing up this flaming astral fiend would get me a good night's sleep.

Wilhelmina rode shotgun, making it look like I was driving a friend's grandmother out on a late-night errand.

The knitting needles reinforced the image. Her hands flew, the shiny blue needles flashing as the streetlights illuminated the car's interior. How those same hands could keep up with her mind, I had no idea. Wilhelmina was in her 70s, with frizzy white hair and wrinkled dark skin. If she had any arthritis problems, she didn't let on.

Of course, I was betting that her knitting bag—the one with a bizarre cat staring out at me—held the modified dagger that my brother had brought from our home dimension. So, if she was getting in regular practice with the tachyon-laced weapon, it was in turn keeping her healthier than she'd otherwise be.

"You feeling up to a second tussle with our new monster?" She asked that between her humming, which was a welcome break from the duplication of the song Luther Vandross was crooning over the radio. Hey, she rides shotgun, she gets radio privileges.

"I'm looking forward to cutting a hole through him big enough to drive my car through, if that's what you mean, so, yeah."

"How's the leg treating you?"

I rolled my eyes. "Really? Another reminder? You guys are the worst support group, you know that, right?"

"Calm down, child." She winked, those brilliant blues full of more mischief that I'd ever seen in my expression in a mirror. And trust me, if you never saw it in my face, you weren't looking closely enough. "Liz told me it malfunctioned and all. I wanted to make sure you were all right using the older model before we put ourselves in danger."

"I'm fine. It'll be great." I tightened my grip on the wheel as I steered us up the 311, back into Arbor Valley. "Probably shouldn't be so snotty. It's the Whisper's suggestion I'm washed up and useless, not yours."

She made a face, a for a moment, I couldn't tell if she'd missed a stitch or wanted to stab the Whisperer—which, frankly, we all did. "That old liar. He's in your head for good, is he? Best we work on that."

"I wouldn't say for good, and it's not like I can text him and say, 'Hey, this thing? It's not working out. I'd like my mental health back,' you know?"

"That ain't what I meant, and you know it. Talk with Ramos, he'll tell you."

"You're gonna say pray on it, aren't you."

"Can't fight the enemy in this kind of war if you've got the wrong weapons, Mercury."

Yeah, yeah. We'd been over this. I didn't belong inside a church. Don't get me wrong—I envied what Ramos called *la paz*—the peace. It had seen him through the worst horrors of being a cop, and that didn't count the insane things he'd experienced when he joined the fight against the monster of the Interstice. Yet he kept his head screwed on straight. "Thanks for the heads-up, Wilhelmina, but I'm doing okay. Really."

"I'll take you at your word, but mind, I won't hesitate to smack you in the back of your head if you step outta line. Especially if we're in the midst of a fight."

"I know you would."

Liz's coordinates told me to turn left onto the next fire road. The numbers were missing, meaning I was relying solely on GPS—without the evil robot voice narration, because if it said one word, I was gonna punch the pulsar stave through my phone.

The car bounced up rutted roads. Crusty, dried-out weeds scraped the undercarriage. Kinda surprising, since the Subaru had a higher clearance than most small cars. But I was not about to complain about foliage damage. My brain provided flashbacks of previous rides getting slashed in half by astral fiends.

Maybe we'd get out and walk the rest of the way to the target.

Liz's face and number appeared on the phone's screen. I tapped the speaker. "Good news, Liz?"

"You're about a half mile away from the tachyon surge, but it's off the road, so I hope you brought some hiking shoes and also don't forget there's probably a lot of ticks still out in the underbrush—"

"Keep feeding whatever the drones pick up." I nudged Wilhelmina. "You ready for a stroll?"

She was already opening the car door. "The less jawing you do, the more oxygen you save for the hike and the fight."

"Everybody's a critic." I snatched the pulsar stave from its holster and followed her.

Wasn't much of a moon but the stars filled the night sky. I was glad for the natural illumination; still, I powered up the stave for extra lighting and, well, I didn't want to stumble upon our fireball friend in the dark.

Wilhelmina withdrew her dagger without comment. The weapon was long as my forearm, with a slender blade forged of Medan metal that, as far as I could tell, cut through most everything in its path. Liz had rigged up a contraption on its hilt that absorbed tachyon particles and infused the dagger with their energy, making it a less-powerful version of the stave that could still imbue Wilhelmina with similar strength and regenerative capabilities as I had.

She carried the genetic marker that let her use Medan weapons. Heck, she'd been Procyon's operative against astral fiends for decades before I came along. And if it wasn't for her, I might have been abandoned to the streets or death after my parents died defending this dimension from the monsters.

I owed her a lot, so I was super glad she was there with me that night.

"Mercury?" Liz was whispering. I guess she was worried I'd have left the phone on speaker while we crept through silent woods toward a possible encounter with a slavering beast. Yeah, I'm not *that* stupid. I had an earbud linked. "The distortion's just a few dozen feet ahead of your position."

Wilhelmina gasped.

"Um, thanks, Liz." I had trouble finding the right words. "Pretty sure we found it."

The forest was mostly junipers and scrub pines. The ones ahead of us were bent into L- and J-shapes, where they weren't growing in bizarre loops. Something had singed their bark. The scent of burnt sugar—sap, I guess—filled the air.

It was the writhing portal in the middle of the clearing that really held my attention.

A great shimmering sphere, cloudy like a fog-socked San Camillo bay in the middle but rimmed with flickering purple-blue light, sat on the ground. Grass sizzled where it touched. Sounds rolled forth— muted roars, muttered words, groaning winds. The air swirled around us, knocking pine needles free.

I brandished the stave. "I'm gonna guess we've got incoming."

"More than likely." Wilhelmina took a deep breath, the dagger held lazily in front of her face. Yellow-white sparks rippled along its blade, across her skin. She relaxed, her body languid, like she was ready to run a marathon. "Let's be sure and give the poor boy a kind welcome."

"Amen to that."

The portal burst into a yawning corridor. It looked like it stretched for miles, yet as it twisted, it had next to no depth. Whether it was an optical illusion or dimensional warping—or maybe both—I had no clue. All I knew was Liz started hollering and I couldn't hear a thing with the suddenly howling wind.

Roasty barreled out like he was late for a train. Trees burst into flame.

But he exited at a 90-degree angle from us because that stupid portal had twisted.

"Intercept him!" Wilhelmina sprinted, dust kicking up behind her shoes.

"Working on it!" I vaulted into a tree, landed on a branch so hard it bounced underfoot, then somersaulted toward the fiend. I wasn't going to let him rampage out of there.

But then I slammed spine-first into a body that

definitely wasn't on fire and wasn't even slimy like an astral fiend.

The owner of the body cried out. We tumbled together, caromed off a tree trunk, and wound up sprawled in the brambles. Which, it should be noted, cut and stung. And me without the supersuit.

What? We were in the middle of a forest. No need for a disguise.

"Unhand me!" The guy's voice was strident yet commanding.

Before I could demand an answer for his interference, I hear a metallic hammer clicking.

"Move, and I'll gift you a gaping hole in your chest," another voice growled. And I do mean growled. Like a bear.

I looked up at a werewolf in a cape, armed with a musket.

What kind of messed up portal was this?

CHAPTER FOUR

In a distant land, in a distant time...

The city haunts my dreams.

It is nothing like a citadel of the five hundred cities of the north. Not a fortress of stone in sight, yet replete with towers that shimmer as the surface of the sea.

Never have I laid eyes upon it. Yet, I awake from the vision sweating, my cloak wrapped around me, sure as the islands soar that I have been there. Such a place of majesty, and yet soaked in misery.

I must have fresh air.

I cling to the rigging on the exposed deck of my cloudship *Northwind* and let the gale tear at my cloak. The air carries water on its currents—salt spray, the lifeblood of the sea. Granted, the sea is hundreds of feet below, a carpet of undulating waves tipped with whitecaps, yet even at this altitude I can imagine myself seaborne.

It is the second smell to reach me that raises alarm. Smoke. The acrid stench comes and goes, a faint odor.

"Must have been a devil of a blaze." Niall Phelan is at *Northwind*'s wheels, guiding the cloudship nearer to the surface. Long red hair whips behind him. Green eyes search the horizon. Lips curl in a sneer, revealing teeth that appear unnaturally sharp, yet which I know can become even sharper should the need arise. "What a stink! It's a whole village consumed, I'd wager."

"Then we'd best make haste. The message indicated they faced annihilation, and I will not be one to let an entire people die."

"Judging by the smell we may be too late." Niall wrinkles his nose. "There's no doubt we will find dead when we arrive."

But he cranks the rise-wheel in any case. *Northwind* plummets, a controlled dive that her reinforced timbers absorb with the barest of groans. I pray the aethershard ensconced deep in the hull does not fracture, as such magic-imbued stones are wont to do when subject to extreme stress. The metal clamps connected to the rise wheel do their job, though, and our descent is that of a dragon on the hunt.

Northwind parts a bank of clouds. I'm shrouded in mist one moment, then out in the sun the next. The sky seeps orange, with purples and pinks shooting through as dusk approaches. The Balaericore Islands sprawl as far as the eye can see, and beyond, great swathes of green and brown snaking across the Atlan

Sea. Would that I had the time to explore their sandy shores, I would take Vesna and Evan to the most beautiful, where she could repose with me in the shade of a palm as our son chases gulls through the sand.

There are few villages to be seen. Farmlands cut through forest, their long rectangles wrapping around hills and encircling lagoons.

A black tendril smudges the sky. "Niall! You see it?"

"That I do, Captain." Niall twists the alter-wheel. *Northwind* banks to starboard, a dagger thrown at its target. "I reckon this is Josarcha. What remains of it."

His assessment is, sadly, accurate. Josarcha village perches on the edge of a hillside, surrounded by palm trees. Thatched roofs peer from beneath a thick canopy of emerald fronds—where they have not been charred beyond recognition. A vast swath of destruction has burned through the homes, leaving few walls intact and fewer people alive. I count three dozen black stains that were once the villagers. Here and there handfuls cluster either for comfort or care.

Cursed creature got to them before we could.

Niall lands *Northwind* in the lagoon a quarter mile away. I let the gangplank slap onto the sandstone outcropping that juts into the water. Fiddler crabs scuttle down barnacled edges and out of the way of our boots.

"Be wary." I load my wheellock pistol and insert

it behind my belt. The falchion sword in its leather sheath slaps against my leg as we walk. "We know not where the beast has taken shelter."

Niall snorts. He lays a musket over his shoulder. "One would think a walking bonfire would be easy to see, whether or not it remains in the depths of the forest."

"Still, I'd rather not happen upon it unprepared."

"Your tone suggests I'm the one who needs preparation."

"No, my tone merely insinuates you are the one who is more likely than not to blithely ignore his surroundings until it is too late and then launch a reckless attack."

"To be fair, we've both been our own fair share of reckless," Niall says.

We trudge up the path to the village, but the moans of the stricken reach us well before we lay eyes upon the ruins at ground level. Fires burn in several homes, having lit trees ablaze.

"It's him!" An elderly woman approaches. Her caftan is scorched, yet her spirit seems undiminished. The glistening burn on her cheek does not prevent her from smiling. "Captain Bowen Cord."

"The one and only," Niall mutters.

I wish I could physically skewer him with the glare I render. "At your service. We received word of an infernal creature threatening your island. I regret we were not able to arrive in time to prevent this tragedy."

"A tragedy of our own making." She points to a clump of soot. My stomach churns. It was once three people, judging by the hazy outline of limbs among the charred remains. "Those fools thought they could tame the beast, make it to do our bidding against corsairs who raid us. They should have known better than to cross paths with a monster that lives in opposition to the will of the Most High."

"Whence has it fled?" Niall traverses the lanes between the homes. He grasps the musket, ready to shoot. He sniffs the air. "There's too much confounded ash. Clouds the scent."

"Ash is its scent," the woman says. "I could but run from it when it attacked us—clambering among the houses like a spider, spreading fire and death in its wake."

A shout grabs our attention. Three young men with buckets cringe in the face of a wall afire, a blaze that has sprung up in the heartbeats since we arrived at the village. Tongues of flame leap onto another stand of trees. The pitiful contents of their pails do little more than turn to steam as they land.

Enough of this.

I stretch forth my hand, fingers spread. Magic suffuses my flesh, yearning to be unleashed, an intense cold pricking my skin as if I have thrust my palm into a pile of nails. One word will release it.

Glacii.

Ice springs forth. The spray, too, becomes steam upon its initial contact with the fire, but I reach deep within myself and open the floodgates to magic. More. Much more. Anything less than a deluge dooms the survivors and their entire island.

The storm spreads across the trees, dousing flames, crystallizing leaves, leaving a sheen on the trunks. Steam fills the air, as does the aroma of wet, burnt wood. I pivot, slowly, boot heels digging into the packed dirt. Widen the spray. Catch every flicker of golden light I see in the dark woods.

Most High, grant the strength to preserve these lives.

I do not know how long I spend extinguishing the fires, only that when Niall's hand drops on my shoulder and he says, "It's done," my knees buckle. The village spins.

And the city takes its place.

I walk streets of stone and ride in carriages of steel. The man at my side is not Niall; I cannot see his face, but I have the impression of joviality and sorrow. Conflict drives him.

My hands are weathered beyond my years. Thoughts escape me, even simple ones... like my name. Yet those hands can still wield a sword, and they do, as the two of us battle unspeakable nightmares.

The dead walk and I slay them...

Niall catches me under an armpit. "Steady, Bowen. I'll not have you fall faint and leave myself without a partner for the hunt. That would be unsporting."

"Kind of you to not deprive me of further adventure." My voice shakes. So. I am still in the village, even if the vision carried me far afield. Tremors wrack my hands as the blue light suffusing them fades. Hold fast. Breathe. My legs regain their stability. I stand straighter.

"Bless you, Captain." The old woman takes my hands. She winces, shakes her fingers free, then attempts the connection again. Surely, she should have known better to touch the hands of a man who's just shown himself to be an ice-summoner. "Your act of kindness will not be forgotten."

"It is the least we could do, though it will not stop us from stalking the beast and ending its depredations." I elbow Niall. "Ready?"

"I would be more ready had I been offered roast pork but given the poor shape of the village I won't press the point."

I give thanks that he keeps his sardonic tone to the barest murmur. To the old woman, I say, "Show us where it went."

A bony finger, gnarled by age as an old tree's branch, points deep into the woods. "Beware the lights, Captain Cord."

I nod, but nestled deep inside the anger I feel toward this mysterious creature is the dark thought: *The only light to be feared is the frozen form I will use to kill it.*

Hours pass. Night falls upon the isles, bringing a warm breeze that makes the forest sigh with each gust. Leaves rustle overhead. Branches creak. The darkness is full of sounds, some of which I can identify and dismiss as harmless, others which fuel my anxieties. At any moment, the beast may emerge from a shadow, ready to burn away our flesh and crisp our bones.

So be it. My heart yearns for revenge, without even knowing a thing about the villagers. It is enough they were innocents.

Yet, there is a caution that restrains my bloodlust. Hate will take me on the wrong path. I have seen too many souls lost in the same manner.

Instead, I watch and wait and pray for guidance.

Niall ducks a low-hanging branch. He pushes aside dangling vines as gently as if he were parting a lace curtain. He is in his element—the silent pursuit. His form crouches, a vulpine silhouette that gives hint to his hidden self.

His fist rises. Halt.

I kneel, six steps behind.

Niall touches the dirt. He rubs it between his fingers, inhales the scent. Without looking back at me, he gestures right with his musket, then lopes into the underbrush.

Very well. Captain or not, I heed his orders in this environment.

Niall's steps fade beneath the forest sounds. Now, I am alone, as surely had I piloted *Northwind* into the sky myself. My grip tightens on the wheellock. I dare not draw the falchion, not yet, not until I know what manner of beast we face.

Yet, from all I have heard, I suspect we are dealing with an arachna-fury.

Reddish light explodes. I squint, shielding my eyes from the sudden dawn, and aim for the source. A shriek pieces the night, chasing away all other sounds with its vehemence. An arachna-fury's cry, I am sure of it, but there is something strained, something immeasurably terrible.

A sharp snarl answers the cry, followed by a musket's ear-shattering report.

I sprint through the forest, crashing through vines. Thorns pull at my cloak. "Niall! Niall, do you have it?"

"Of all the goblin-brained things to ask! Of course I have it! Lend me aid before it has me!"

I burst into a clearing, one as broad as *Northwind*'s deck, and recently made larger by the felling of a dozen trees. Niall brandishes his katana, the slender blade glittering in the firelight. His musket is slung on a strap over his shoulder.

But all that I notice only in the periphery of my vision. The beast ahead of us holds my full attention.

It may have begun its wretched life as an arachna-fury, but some dark purpose has warped its form. There is a bulbous body, inflated from the natural shape of a giant spider, yet the hide has become slathered with ichor. Flame still issues forth, yet it consumes the eight legs, which have gone limp and writhing like the appendages of a kraken. Those tentacles slash at Niall, who rolls to one side and hacks at the nearest limb with his katana.

The keening wail threatens to shatter my eardrums. I take advantage of the wound to fire.

Smoke obscures my vision. The shot pierces the hide, the gash issuing forth a stream of thick, blue... sludge. Not only is the shot effective in striking my enemy, it brings his gaze toward me and away from Niall.

Bile rises at the sight of the mutated face. It is as if a mad painter has smeared a portrait of an arachna-fury, blotting eight beady eyes into three orbs glowing red, and stretched mandibles into a yawning maw filled with more fangs than grains of sand on the shore. The beast looms over me, thrashing the air, flinging sparks and embers into the forest canopy.

I thrust my pistol into my belt and throw ice between us.

A wall extends from the ground, building upon itself until a crackling barrier taller than a cloudship's mast hems in our adversary inside a horseshoe shape.

"Freeze him!" Niall's voice is a low, guttural growl, a misshapen version of his mellow tones. His body twists in grotesque fashion, muscles growing, limbs lengthening. Face and mouth stretch into that of a fox's, replete with red and white fur. "Freeze the fiend!"

"That is my goal!" I lift my arms, raising the sleet spray until it arches over in a frozen dome.

The monster breaks through as easily as if he were

tearing paper, yet he gets stuck halfway through.

"Shark's blood!" Niall lunges for the nearest appendage, ready to sever it without care for his well-being.

"Stand fast!" I snap. "I can seal him in!"

My body thrums with magic. There's not an ounce of flesh that doesn't resonate. I cannot tap into its source forever, though, and a distant part of my mind wonders if an ice-summoner has ever frozen solid.

Even as I contend against the beast, holding it back as best I can as scalding heat assails me, sounds slacken. Its thrashing slows, as does Niall's swordplay. The sleet stabbing from my hands becomes lackadaisical.

And the city fills my thoughts yet again.

The visions are sharper, clearer. I could be walking the foreign streets...

As I have before?

No. Not possible. I have never in my life seen a place as strange. And yet, I cannot escape the feeling of familiarity.

Stars wink out. The nighttime sky swirls, a whirlpool of light and smoke. And from the pitch black at the center...

Trees?

Upside down trees.

Sparks shoot from their crowns, up into the sky—or down toward us.

The ice wall shatters. The whirlpool drags the trees from their roots, both above and around me, and pulls shards apart.

Niall tumbles end over end, flung from the ground toward—another clearing. Another forest.

Two places become one, and in that instant, I see the monster stretched between realms.

I am flung between here and there. No matter for what I reach, I cannot latch on. I flail, useless.

The mad scramble ends when I smack into Niall, who must have reverted to his human form, for the vulpex is sans fur. But no. Not Niall. This man is too lithe, too short. His outcry is not the outrage I'd associate with my friend.

"Unhand me!" I push free.

Niall is suddenly there, standing guard. He brandishes the musket at this interloper. Never mind how he came to be in our midst on Josarcha.

Hold. The trees are stunted pines, blackened by fire. They're nothing like the swaying palms. And the ground is too dry. And the sky—

The stars are wrong. Some too bright, others too dim, none in the proper place.

Niall helps me up. He is still the vulpex, his claws extended. "Shall I shoot the whelp? Or save ammunition for the monster, wherever it has fled?"

"Let's let him live for the time being. I for one—" Words fail me as the young man's face resolves in the evening light. I have never seen him before, yet I know him, somehow, as surely as I know Niall.

"You keep staring, I'm gonna have to have the cops get a restraining order." His tone drips sarcasm.

That voice rings in my mind. Suddenly, the name is there. This is the man from the city—from the vision. The one whom I helped slay the undead. "Mercury?" I say.

His eyes widen. "Oh great," he mutters. "Another one."

CHAPTER FIVE

Okay, to be fair, he wasn't a werewolf. He was red and white, not the slate gray I'd expect from a man who transformed into a shaggy monster animal.

So, a were-fox?

But that wasn't the problem. The problem was the monster had vanished.

Super. And to make matters worse, the random bearded guy wearing the cape was staring at me like he was expecting me to—I don't know, explode or something.

"What has happened to the beast?" The were-fox snarled his words. Which I guess was easy for him, seeing as how his face was full of canine teeth.

"He's standing right in front of me," I said. "If you're talking about the astral fiend that's on fire, then I don't know."

"Don't take that tone with me!" Were-fox shifted the aim of his musket.

"Mind your manners, now." Wilhelmina snuck in from the shadows. Her amped-up dagger hovered by the critter's rib cage, ready to filet him. "Let's all not commit any undue violence, hear?"

Nice intervention, but I was too fired up to back down. "Listen, man. If this is some weird combo of fantasy LARPing mixed with Revolutionary re-enactment, I think that's pretty cool, but why don't you take your popgun and go home. I've got real terrors to deal with. And I'm not talking about the funky smell coming off your fur."

"Of all the dragon-chewed goblin filth... You'll close that mouth of yours for good." He drew back on the musket's hammer.

Cute. I willed power into the pulsar stave, enough to get it glowing like the sun, then touched its tip to the barrel. The metal turned cherry-red, molten. The end sloughed off, leaving sizzling patches in the dirt.

"That's enough, Niall." The bearded guy pushed the were-fox away and, surprisingly, the were-fox didn't literally bite his head off. Niall just grimaced as he inspected the ruined musket. "This lad is no threat to us. Nor is his elder."

Wilhelmina snorted and rolled her eyes.

Lad? I made a face. "You part of this Renaissance fair, too?"

The pulsar stave lit up the bearded visage. His expression was way too familiar to belong to some dude who'd just dropped out of a portal. Then, the guy smiled. "Mercury. I cannot explain how it us, but it is good to see you."

"Yeah... Okay." I tapped my earpiece. Enough of fun time with strangers. I needed answers. "Liz, you there?"

"Mercury! What's going on? When the portal opened, I thought it was a second rip like the kind that dumped out the fiery astral fiend, but the tachyon pulses were off the chart and the gravitational distortion—!"

"Easy, Liz. Tell me where it went."

"Okay. Okay." Deep, whooshing breaths hissed through my earpiece. When Liz continued, she sounded calmer. "It's hop-skipping around the woods."

"How very bucolic." Loredana's dry tones cut in. "Mercury, return to your car. We'll keep you apprised of the situation and determine an exit point. It appears the creature is circling toward the highway."

"On it." I started away from the clearing, but stopped, one foot propped on a smoldering log. "What about these guys?"

"You'll need to specific."

"I know the drone's up there." I waved skyward. A tiny blinking light responded. "You're seeing them, right?"

Niall pitched his ruined weapon into the brush. He brandished a ninja sword. Really? Because I hadn't had enough of bladed weapons lately? "We'd best continue the hunt, Bowen. This one seems good only for prattle."

I pointed a finger. "Hey, listen, fur-face—"

The rest of my insult evaporated as Niall turned into a man. I mean, his fur retracted, his features melted, and next thing I knew, a handsome red-headed guy in baggy white shirt and brown pants stood there. He had a cape, too, because why not?

"Well if that don't beat all," Wilhelmina murmured.

"We can be of assistance," the bearded guy— Bowen, apparently—said. "We have pursued the strange beast to this same place, though we have no inkling how we came to be here."

"Yeah, well, give Liz a sec and she'll find a couple inklings." I ran a hand through my hair. Sweat slicked my palm. It was criminal that it was still this hot so late in the evening. Didn't help that Bowen's unnerving stare was growing more and more recognizable with each second that ticked by.

"Mercury," Loredana said. "You and Wilhelmina must get moving."

"I know, I know." Sounded petulant, but hey, I figured it was better than throwing a "Yes, dear," across the radio waves, mostly because I'd seen how well Loredana could shoot. Seriously, though. Enough of this standing around. But what was I gonna do with these jokers? Downside, they popped out of a portal, which was never a good thing, unless, you know, they were family. Plus side? They had swords. And one guy could transform.

"Fire." Niall sniffed the air like was still in fox-mode.

He was right. A tree not thirty feet had burst into flame.

"Confound it all." Bowen sighed and aimed his palm at the fire like he was gonna tell it to get lost. He whispered a word and blue light suffused his whole hand, pulsating down his wrist and under his sleeve.

He sprayed ice on the newborn blaze like he was a human fire extinguisher.

I stared at the clumps of ice that weighed down the branches. Then I pointed at Bowen and Niall. "Okay, never mind the last three minutes. I'm Mercury Hale. This is Sherry Jean Crown—likes to be called Wilhelmina. Nice to meet you. Let's go kill us a flaming meatball."

Gotta hand it to those guys—they could sprint. I scrambled as best I could over loose dirt, patches of sand, and almost faceplanted when I tripped over a stray root. Who put that thing there? Wilhelmina was right beside me, handling every obstacle with an ease borne of her absorbing energy from the modified Medan dagger. Bowen and Niall, though, ran like they were stars of their high school track teams back in the day—though I had a sneaking suspicion neither of them had a clue what a high school was.

You should have seen their faces when I hopped into the Subaru.

Bowen eased into the passenger seat. He tapped

the roof overhead. "Cramped."

"It isn't roomy, but it's fast." I gunned the engine, not waiting to see if Niall had figured out the deal. "Get in!"

The big lug smacked his head on the doorframe. He snarled in a manner that sounded startlingly like an actual animal. "I won't be confined in such a cramped carriage."

"Quit your jawing and get in!" Wilhelmina shoved him. Her door slammed. "Lordy. You and Mercury could heat up a hot air balloon with all the excess gas."

"Remove your hands, crone!" Niall glared at her. "Bowen, this contraption has no horses. What am I supposed to do, wish for an aethershard?"

"It does have a wheel." Bowen peered at the ignition switch. "Is that key what accesses the magic?"

I grinned. "Nah. That's the pedals."

I popped it into drive and sped down the road.

There was another meaty thud. Niall yelped. Must've hit his head again. Either that or Wilhelmina walloped him for calling her crone. "If this pup kills me, I'll cut out his spleen!"

"Shut up and belt up!" I snapped.

We skidded out onto the highway, headlights illuminating a dump truck as we slid into the next lane. I really thought our lives were gonna end in twisted metal and the deafening blare of a car horn, which would be a terrible way to go after everything I'd experienced. So, the narrow miss was super.

"Mercury!" Liz again. "I've got the fiend. It's headed toward the city."

Perfect. Because why would it roll out of town, away from the places where it could do the most damage? I cranked on the wheel, slammed the brakes, and put us unto reverse. The ensuing turn was so sharp I thought we'd all end up with whiplash. "On it!"

It wasn't but a minute before we saw it, leaping from culvert to culvert at what had to be 40 or 50 mph. That made it easier to keep up. Not that I was happy the critter could teleport itself from Point A to Point B just like its less fiery relatives.

"Get me nearer, and I can stop the creature." Bowen rapped on the passenger side window. "Shall I break this, or does it open of its own accord?"

Something about the way he was speaking—and the fact that he wasn't freaking out about riding in my car—was ringing a bell. I lowered the window with a flip of a switch.

"Thank you." He stuck his hands outside and hauled himself through the gap where a nice, safe pane of glass used to be.

"That's not a bad idea." The admiration was plain in Wilhelmina's voice.

"You stay put. And, hey! Bowen! What'd I just say about seat belts?" The car rabbited toward the center line. A passing pickup honked, and I jerked the wheel swerving us back the other way.

"We have to slay the beast, and since your carriage

does not hold any cannons—"

"And you melted my bloody musket," Niall growled from behind me.

"—I must take action to end its rampage." With that, Bowen was out of the car, his cloak discarded on the seat. The last thing I saw were a pair of very cool leather boots with big old cuffs, pirate style, vanishing into the dark.

Something pressed down on the roof. I swear there was the indent of a shoe right over my head.

"Shark's blood." Niall contorted himself, his foot up near his ear, so he could slide into the front passenger seat. "If you'd but left me my gun, we'd be able to end this battle all the sooner."

"Hate to disappoint you, but this is a car chase." I wound my window down. We were a couple car lengths behind the fiery fiend. I charged the pulsar stave and separated one half, letting the other drop into my lap. Yikes! That was cold. "Quit whining about that stupid gun because you're the only one without a toy at the party."

"Get me near enough and my fangs will do more than a musket ball or your lightning stick."

Lightning stick? I sneered and thrust the stave half out the window. Check this out.

A blast of yellow-white energy crackled through the night air, lending daylight to our stretch of the highway. Struck that stupid fiend right in its flaming rear end—not that it actually had one.

Sizzling hide sheared off, which was great, until it

spattered across the windshield. Reflex forced me to turn on the wipers and, yeah, I added some spray. All that did was make it about a hundred times harder to see.

"Good shot!" Wilhelmina's hand slapped my shoulder. "But I have to throw in my two cents with our hairy new friend—drop us off so we can get to stabbing."

But my attack did the trick. Too well. The fiend halted in midair. I slammed on the brakes, tires squealing, and put the car into a spin. Niall howled from the passenger seat, one hand one the door and the other squeezing my shoulder so hard I thought he'd break a bone. Wilhelmina laughed.

A sword tip cut through the roof. Any closer to my face and I wouldn't have had to shave for the next week.

Huh. I knew I'd seen a blade that shape somewhere before—

We slid sideways underneath the fiend as fiery tentacles lashed down. Asphalt bubbled. The car's tires didn't like that. Felt like I was driving over the wrong side of a giant sheet of duct tape. Flame melted the passenger rear view mirror.

That's what I got for bringing my car into this mess. Again.

And what in the world was that Bowen guy waiting for?

The night suddenly lit up with that blue light. Frost crept over the roof, down through the open windows, and crystalized on the windshield. I leaned over the steering wheel.

Bowen crouched on the hood. Ice streamed from both hands, pummeling the fiery fiend. Its screams rattled the glass and vibrated the whole car. Tentacles flopped at its sides, turned from flaming weapons into limp, charcoaled noodles.

Now *that* was impressive.

The rest of us didn't need invites. We leap from the car. I stepped in hot asphalt and yelped, because yeah, I could feel that through the soles of my shoes. That didn't stop me from lunging for the fiend's useless appendages, the energy blades from the pulsar staves searing them off with clean, sweeping cuts.

"Bowen!" Niall wrenched the sword from my roof and threw it.

It seemed to float through the air, and in that suspended moment, my brain put it together—it was shaped just like the one from Liz's apartment. The one she'd lent to me when Skipper and I needed weaponry a few months back during our fight against Alexander Arkwright and a horde of undead corpse-fiends. A falchion, she'd called it.

Skipper?

Bowen snatched the weapon while in a spin, ducking an incoming tentacle, and brought it up with a savage cry. He thrust the blade deep into the monster's hide, burying it up to the hilt. Thick, bluish-black ooze soaked his hands.

The fiend shrieked until I thought my brains were

gonna bleed out my ears. But it was a good sound. My favorite. Because it meant that guy's time was short.

Instead of sublimating into a film that would eventually evaporate, though, the thing's eyes burned with a literal fire. That fire didn't stay put. No such luck. It spread from the eyes, like rain streaming down a window, except it ran in rivulets all over the thing's body. Tentacles regrew. As in, super-fast.

Worse, the fire streams congregated around Bowen's blade.

Metal started to glow.

"Clouds above!" Bowen wrenched the sword free. Ichor spattered his shirt, eating holes in the fabric. He slipped off the hood.

"Get back and let me ruin the foul creature!" Niall stood astride his fallen pal, the ninja sword flashing red as it reflected the flames. "I'll gut every last inch of its entrails!"

Tentacles swarmed around him, newly ignited. Idiot was gonna get himself killed. I rejoined the pulsar stave and slammed one end into the pavement. The explosion of energy vaulted me far over the fiend, nearly to the treetops, letting me somersault through the rest of the fiery tentacles. Had to find a clear landing spot...

There.

I landed atop its hide.

My leg buckled.

No! Not now!

I collapsed, the pulsar stave askew. Its energies tore open the fiend's hide but didn't penetrate nearly deep enough to kill it.

And it knew. Boy, did it ever.

A searing tentacle wrapped around my waist. It felt a thousand times worse than touching my fingers to a hot baking sheet fresh from the over. Only the stave's power, absorbed into my body, kept it from melting the flesh clean from my bones.

Something slammed into me and I thought I was gonna have the life drained from me, either before or after I was burned alive. But it wasn't superheated astral fiend tentacle hide. It was Wilhelmina.

She and I wound up in a ditch, sprawled in leaves and dirt. Steam rose around us. I couldn't breathe. Someone was driving a knife through my leg, I was sure of it.

The fiend turned on us. Three tentacles slashed through the darkness, flaming whips that signaled major pain.

Niall was there, a red-white blur with a sword. He lopped off the ends of all three with one swipe. Heck of an intercession.

The monster pummeled him with the stumps. Knocked him onto his backside. I figured the fiend was ready for its next meal. Instead it contracted in a whip-crack of thunder and purple light, dragged into a gash of darkness so black I thought I was gonna fall into it even though it was above me. A sudden wind thrashed the trees and bounced the car on its tires.

The sonic boom tipped the Subaru on its side and the fiend was gone.

Boots shuffled on loose asphalt. Bowen staggered to us, dragging his sword. "How did you fare?"

Niall held out a hand that morphed from red- and white-furred into human as Bowen helped him to his feet. He slapped Bowen on the shoulder. "Not dead. Not yet."

"Though you did try your hardest to remedy that, I see." Bowen cracked a smiled.

Niall chuckled. "It does get the heart up, doesn't it?"

"You two are insane." I propped myself up with the pulsar stave.

"Take it easy, now." Wilhelmina had my arm around her shoulder. "You ain't in no shape to go hauling after that thing."

She wasn't wrong. I needed the crutch, because my prosthetic leg had melted. All that remained was a plastic and metal mush that had hardened into a lump like a green toy army man exposed to a pyro kid's matches. "The astral fiend's gone, and if it can't be killed, we're in deep trouble."

"Never met a beast what can't be slain," Niall grumbled.

"Yeah, well, I never met a young version of a guy I already knew, so we're two for two in crazy new experiences." I let Bowen help me stand. Made sure to look him square in the face. Younger, sure. The beard was a rich brown, the skin free of the wrinkles of old age. What weathering there was seemed to have been put in place by sun. The eyes, though... and the lilt of his puzzled smile. "I don't believe it. No wonder you knew my name."

"Mercury Hale." Bowen shook his head. "I do know you, don't I?"

"Sort of. I think." I prodded his chest. "You're Skipper, all right, but about thirty years too young."

CHAPTER SIX

I sat on the edge of the exam bed, trying not to think about the gouges and scrapes marring the side of my car.

The throbbing ache of my stump made those concerns easier to ignore. That leg, though. I glared down at the space where the rest of the limb should have been. It would have been easier to blame my stumble at the farm stand on glitchy tech. But this? This time it was nothing but operator error. Just me and the simple prosthetic.

Loredana set a hand on my knee. Anybody else who'd tried that would have been in danger of getting amputated. Her touch seemed to sap away the pain. "It will take time."

"You sure you can't mind read?"

She smirked at our long-standing inside joke. "I don't require telepathy to read your heart, Mercury. Recovering from the loss of a limb is never easy. You've only been traveling that road for a few months."

"I get that. But I also take way less time to heal than the average bear, as Yogi would say. I assumed, I guess, that would translate to physical therapy." I shook my head. "There's darker moments when I wish I'd never made the decision that I did."

"Impossible. Then you'd be dead."

"The thought had crossed my mind." I smiled and tapped the side of my head.

"You gave up much. There isn't a person here who doesn't respect you for the risks taken and sacrifices made." She leaned in, her hand shifting to my chest. "Because your heart is in the right place."

"And Doc Arne would confirm it, too."

She rolled her eyes, but her smile didn't leave. "Give yourself credit, at least: You're facing threats at near-peak performance far faster than Dr. Becker anticipated."

"Yes, and Dr. Becker would keep his patient confined to civilian duty if he wasn't constantly overruled by people with no regard for human decency." Arne Becker had materialized at the end of the bed as if he'd teleported—which would totally fit into the realm of possibility given we had a guy who could do exactly that on Procyon's payroll. Lithe like an athlete, Doc Arne sported a beard that would've better suited a Millennial barista or a Shattered Mug customer complaining about the lack of avocado toast. He had enough product slicking his hair down he could have incapacitated an astral fiend with the smell alone. He force-fed notes into his tablet with a stylus.

"One problem, Doc." I pantomimed shooting. "I'm not human."

He scowled. "You're human enough. I don't care which dimension you're from. I've got an oath and you've got to be more careful."

"You bet, Mom. Did you bring me anything besides your sunny disposition? Like, good news? And a spare leg?"

He gestured at a nearby table. Yep, there was the glitchy but souped-up version, the one that could siphon the pulsar stave's energy and feel near as close to a real limb as the lost one. It looked like Liz had printed a new cover; the starry casing had cleaner, sharper edges. Here was hoping the interior was equally upgraded. "We'll re-fit you in a moment. Ms. Lark wanted my report."

"Sure. On my passengers." I glanced over my shoulder. Bowen and Niall sat on adjacent beds. Doc Arne had gotten Bowen a black T-shirt with a red dragon emblem in the center of the chest. It was from the stash of donated clothing Procyon kept on hand for me in case a tussle with an astral fiend resulted in a wardrobe malfunction. This one was from some writing conference about realm-making, back East.

Bowen had his fingers interlaced and was staring at the ceiling. Niall, still clad in his grimy white tunic, tapped a boot on the bed's wheels. He caught me looking, glowered, and increased both the tempo and volume of the tapping. His fingers dipped inside his shirt collar. There was a pendant hanging there, glass framed copper. Couldn't figure out why he had a feather sandwiched between those tiny panes. A keepsake?

Doc Arne waved his tablet at the pair. "Those men are also human, and they're also not from our dimension."

"You want a prize for that deduction?"

"I want you to close your mouth before I suture it shut."

I looked at Loredana, who seemed to be fighting off a full-fledged grin. She shrugged, her not-so-subtle version of, "I told you so." I made a gesture like I was zipping my mouth shut and flicked away an imaginary key.

"Their bloodwork comes back as human," Arne said. "But I found markers not dissimilar to yours."

Loredana jumped in with, "Not dissimilar?"

"I'm sure Liz can get into the particulars of trans-dimensional components, or whatever it is she's calling these bizarre genetic structures. Let's leave it at this: Neither man is from this world, nor are they from Meda, but they're from the same place as one another."

"Presumably from which our modified astral fiend originated."

"Bowen talked about fighting it near a village on an island." The words burst forth from my lips like a flood from a broken dam. That was probably the longest I'd gone being mute. "Which makes no sense because I was fighting it in the middle of the forest. Or at least, a copy of it."

"Again, that's for Liz." Doc Arne made a face at the readouts on his tablet that most men reserved for insults said about their moms. "But back to your other question—"

"He's Skipper, right? Only younger."

Arne nodded. No snotty rejoinder. Just a dumb bob of the head.

"Okay, that makes no sense, and understand that gets put on a list of a whole lot of stuff that makes no sense." I glanced between Arne and Loredana, waiting for a brilliant explanation from either or both. Zilch. "Skipper was old—okay, not ancient, but no sword-swinging spring chicken. This guy, Bowen, he can't be much older than me. Late 20s? Maybe 30? If you're saying they're the same person, then old Bowen came here without his memory months ago before young Bowen showed up—but young Bowen knows my name!"

"I'll not pretend to understand any better than anyone in this room." Loredana folded her arms. "However, there is evidence of various bridges through the Interstice that breach not only space but time. The parallel Earth, for example, is slightly off from ours."

Don't even ask about that one. I ran a hand through my hair quickly, because if I slowed down, I'd have pulled out enough to go bald. "Man. Okay, maybe we ought to let them out of quarantine."

"Sticking them on beds in the corner of this bunker doesn't come close to qualifying as quarantine," Arne grumbled. "Though they should be. Who knows what microbes they brought from wherever their home is?"

"I'm joking, Arne."

"I'm not." He shrugged. "But what do I know? I'm only a doctor."

He stormed deeper into the cramped confines of the makeshift infirmary. Really thought he was gonna tack on, "Not a Tracking specialist" or some other job title to his snide comment, but I had no clue whether or not he was a Trekkie. Couldn't blame him for his increased irritation, though. The room was nowhere near as bright and sanitary as the cool, white room infirmary of Procyon's Tower Three. This really was a bunker, all faded concrete and metal that was painted pasty green. Here was hoping none of said paint was lead-based.

Doc Arne snapped commands at a young man and woman in white lab coats, both scurrying like scolded puppies in his wake. Which left Loredana and me alone with our dimensionally displaced duo.

"So." I pulled on the repaired prosthetic leg. It hummed for a moment as a sheen of golden light raced down its sides. "Let's do this."

She gestured for me to take the lead and smiled.

Still wasn't used to that. In the aftermath of our showdown with Alexander Arkwright—and everyone's acknowledgement that I had two other

"You and Mercury were fighting the same creature in two dimensions at the same 'time,' if we use the term loosely."

"Yeah, and trust me, an astral fiend is plenty of trouble when you're tangling with it solo in one location." The ache returned to my leg. I winced and shifted my weight.

"Astral fiend." Bowen frowned. "You mean the arachnafury?"

I grinned at Loredana. "I don't know what that is, but it's a cooler name."

"Indeed, but I find the arachna- prefix troubling."

"Giant spider." Niall waggled his fingers in a creepy-crawly fashion. "With a thick hide set aflame. Born of magma and corrupt magic."

"That is definitely way cooler," I said.

Loredana pinched the bridge of her nose and closed her eyes. "Focus, please, gentlemen."

My phone rattled in my pocket. The earbud was tucked below it, so I answered the old-fashioned way. "Yello."

"Hey, Mercury do you have a sec? I've got an update on Roasty—or the fire fiend. Whatever it is. I think maybe I need to program Cyril with a fancier designation, so we don't get confused."

"We'll be right up. And I think I can help with that last part." I winked at Loredana. "Call it an astral fury."

"Oooh, I like it! See ya!"

I started for the door, basking in the minor win.

Liz must've thought I had only Loredana in tow—though to be fair, Loredana's long-legged stride put her through the door to Tracking six steps before me. Anyway, she stopped in mid-guzzle of her giant plastic cup of iced tea.

Bowen and Niall entered as part of our entourage.

"Remarkable." Bowen peered at the bevy of screens. If the tech geeks minded a swashbuckling monster fighter looming over their shoulders as they worked, they showed no outward signs. "These words move upon stained glass. This manner of magic—it is the same as the relic you carry?"

I spun the compact form of the pulsar stave end over end and caught it. "You mean this?"

"No, the smaller one."

"Oh. My phone?" I waggled it. "Yeah, I can call pretty much anyone in the continental US. Or farther. Probably costs more… Well, and with the Internet I can find any information about anything, you know?"

Bowen moved his mouth but had no audible words for me.

"Parlor tricks are nice," Niall said. "But if you've never seen a dragon tear a flying warship in half as easily as a child plucking a blade of grass, I'm not to be easily impressed."

I shrugged. "Does Smaug count? I think he just went after a village, though."

"Let's have your status report, Elizabeth." Loredana's flat tone was a warning bell—time to get back to business.

I had to nudge Liz, though, because she sat at her desk with her chin propped against her fist as she leaned forward in her chair. Iced tea dripped from around the straw of her tilted cup.

"Hey," I hissed. "Liz." No good. I waved my hand in front of her face.

She sighed, unblinking. What was so impressive about the map?

Oh. Right. It was the musclebound guy standing in front of the map.

"Elizabeth."

Loredana snapped out the word. Liz reacted like it was a cattle prod. "Yes. Yes! I can zoom in to show the whole United States or down to one lady picking her nose on a San Camillo sidewalk."

"All well and good, but perhaps a fix on the location of the astral fury—if I must use the name—will suffice."

"Oh. Um, about that..." Liz swiped through menus on her giant tablet of a screen. The map of America blurred, resolving only when the familiar tilted grid of San Camillo's streets took its place. A pair of red dots appeared. "Here's where Mercury fought the astral fury, first at the farm stand, then deeper in the forest."

"Where is it now?" Niall lifted his chin as he inspected the map. "Can your window-map show us?"

"That's the problem. It isn't staying still." Liz tapped her screen.

More than twenty dots speckled San Camillo and the surrounding countryside.

"This complicates matters," Loredana muttered.

"Shark's blood." Niall put his hands on his hips. "Are we to journey to each one? That could take days!"

"Nah. A really long day, maybe…" I rubbed my face. "Are these where it's showed up?"

"They're tachyon spikes, yeah, but I can't tell if the astral fury has actually stayed in our dimension or hopped into the next. Each happened with fifteen minutes of you guys' last fight with it." Liz chewed her straw. "I mean, I thought it was going to reappear, so I tried repositioning the drones to get clean tracking data. Nothing ever happened."

"It lurks out there, waiting for us." Bowen joined Niall at the map. "What say you? If I get you down wind, can you track it?"

Niall sneered. Those teeth shouldn't have been that sharp. "Near enough to carve myself a keepsake before I gut it."

"Good man." Bowen slapped his shoulder. "If this young lady can aid us with her wizardry, we may yet destroy the beast."

"Hey, guys?" I tapped the pulsar stave on Liz's desk. "Here's the deal—we can't do anything until Liz can pinpoint when and where it's going to next show up. I'm not traipsing around my city with an ice-mage and his shapeshifting buddy, sword and all, until we have a plan of attack. Got it?"

"Mind your tongue, whelp." The top of my head was just below Niall's nose, which meant he could glower down at me. "I'll remind you there's but one captain I follow."

"Steady on." Bowen put a hand to his friend's shoulder. "The lad's correct. Perhaps our best option is rest. It's been a long night—or day, now, I suppose. Would you have anything akin to a tavern at which we could rest?"

"My place." Yeah, okay, I said no taking them into the city, but that was on a monster hunt. This was door-to-door. "We could all use a recharge."

"We'll keep you apprised." Loredana kissed me full on the lips. "Text if you need anything."

"Likewise."

I headed for the door, stopping only when Liz said, "Um… Ice-mage?"

Bowen said something that sounded like "Glassy," and pointed two fingers at Liz's iced tea. Frost turned the cup white, freezing it to the desk.

Liz yelped. She broke it free, the ice cracking.

"Heaven help us all," Loredana murmured.

"That is the idea." Niall gave her a cheery salute as we left.

CHAPTER SEVEN

The thing I wanted most was a good night's sleep. Instead my restless brain treated me to a night filled with terrible dreams, hideous images brimming with death and destruction, featuring my incompetence. Bonus: Sweat-soaked T-shirt and a big old drool spot on the pillow when I woke up.

"Coffee," I moaned.

My house guests didn't take that as the cry for help it so obviously was. I mean, in all fairness, that was because they were both dead to the world. Bowen could have been ready to slide into a coffin, his cloak serving as a blanket, boots kicked off at the end of the couch. Niall was curled on his side, on the floor. I was pretty sure the neighbors were gonna start pounding on my door if his snoring kept up.

Thankfully, the phone buzzed. Bad news? Not Loredana offering a ride to a well-deserved latte.

"Mercury? I need you in Wells Heights."

"Hey, Ramos." I rubbed at my face, as if I could

scrub intelligence and awareness into my near-comatose brain. "No perky greeting? You have to sleep on the couch last night? Because I got a guy who beat you to it."

"I was up early when Stan Bradley called in the report of three burned bodies."

The last word launched me out of bed. I marched into the living room and kicked the couch. "Hey. Hey! Get up."

"Trouble?" Bowen's eyes were bleary, but he sounded and looked way too awake when compared with yours truly.

"More than likely." I swung a second kick at Niall's shin, but he caught it. No kidding. One moment, passed out like a puppy after he'd gorged on his kibble. Then next, bolt upright, iron grip latched around my ankle. I tottered, arms flailing.

"Mercury?" Ramos' voice did this neat trick where it could sound like he was ready to throttle me through a phone's speaker.

"One sec!"

Niall bared his teeth. What, did he forget the human versions weren't supposed to be so sharp? "Try it again and I'll use the katana's blade."

"Hey. Easy. Heel." I got balanced well enough to break free. "Ramos, still there?"

"Am I interrupting a party? This isn't a serious enough matter for you?"

"Relax, will you? These guys are—" I blew out a breath, watching as Bowen and Niall got their boots on. Unfamiliarity with twenty-first century San Camillo didn't stop them from figuring out where I kept the food. Skipper's memories probably informed Bowen what a fridge was. "New allies. I think. But never mind. I take it you're calling because wildfires aren't nibbling at San Camillo's trendiest neighborhood?"

"Not unless they can hop eight miles from the nearest reported blaze and light three people plus the surrounding patch of ground without burning a path there."

"That's what I was afraid of. Be there in a few." I hung up.

"We are prepared to meet the fiend." Bowen strapped on his sword belt.

"It'd be a better match if someone hadn't destroyed our best gun." He glared at me while positioning his scabbard.

"Hold up." I interposed myself between my eager sword-wielding duo and the door. "Bowen's got the right gear—T-shirt and all. But Niall, you're still sporting the cosplay."

"This?" He plucked at white fabric. "There's nothing wrong with my tunic."

"Not unless you're blind and can't smell," I muttered. "Leave out the stench and you've still got astral fury... gunk on it."

"There's hardly time to clean it." Bowen tried to squeeze around me for the door.

"Easy." I drew the pulsar stave. "Let's get him

properly attired."

They backed into the living room as I rummaged about for another shirt. Bowen seemed bemused, waiting there with his arms folded.

Niall growled, "I'd rather have a new gun."

"One thing at a time!" I snapped.

Got Niall a gray T-shirt sporting the blue crest and Triforce from *The Legend of Zelda* games. It was two sizes too small. I mean, the guy could win the beach bod competition if he'd shown up three months ago. Pretty sure my shirt was never gonna fit me again. I made them both leave their cloaks behind, too, and carry their swords as unobtrusively as possible.

Not too bad when we had to climb into the Subaru. Only got a couple of odd looks from passers-by. Of course, one of said looks came from a teen whose ears were pierced in six places, had blue hair, and was carrying a fuzzy white Pomeranian that could've gotten beaten in a fight with a squirrel. Weird was relative.

What Ramos thought of my entourage was evident the moment my battered Subaru pulled up to the scene of the crime in Wells Heights.

San Camillo Police Department had the entire cul-de-sac blocked off. The fact that they waved me through without a second look was testament to how serious the situation was. Ramos must have radioed ahead and let the patrol officers know I was on my way—but seriously, what did that conversation sound like? Mercury's gonna show up in a car that looks like it should be on a sleazy salesman's back lot, with two strange guys riding passenger?

For one thing, the car didn't belong in the neighborhood. McMansions abounded, so much so that I took two wrong turns before GPS guided me into the correct cul-de-sac. And seeing it perched between a pair of Lexuses—Lexi?—further reinforced that it had seen a rough night with the scrapes raked across the hood, roof, and especially the doors. Don't forget about the melted rear-view mirror. I swore the Lexuses edged away from the Subaru the same way you ease aside from the crazy guy talking to himself at the bus stop.

But I guess after monsters and zombies and an evil artifact hellbent on drowning an entire city, the three of us weren't that big of a deal to the cops.

Bowen, Niall, and I headed for the yellow police line tape. They brought their swords, because, of course they did.

"I suppose this is better than having it cut in half." A smirk teased the corners of Ramos' lips.

"Stick to the policing and leave the quips to the veteran." I tipped up my sunglasses. Ramos did so simultaneously, and I won't lie, I felt pretty cool in that moment.

At least I did until we took in the scene. The astral fury had brought death into a broad swath of emerald green lawn that was immaculate except for the huge burnt patch big enough to park two cars end to end inside. Three bodies were in the middle. Bodies? More like crispy mummies. Yeah, even though they were charred clear to the bone, I could tell they'd been desiccated—as in, drained of life, an astral fiend's preferred method of feeding.

Ramos leaned in. "Are these two Procyon's newest recruits? Because if they are, I'm going to introduce them to city statutes regarding the carrying of weapons."

"Little late to worry about permits, Ramos. Besides they're not in your jurisdiction." I texted Liz, <At the scene. Drones coming?>

"So... recruits from far afield." Ramos peered at them.

"Yeah. The bearded guy? Skipper."

Ramos frowned. "That can't be."

"Can and is. Doc Arne confirms it."

Niall's head cocked. He glanced at the sky. "A cloudship approaches. And yet—too small. Only the fae could ride it."

Took me a minute to understand what he was muttering about, but sure enough, one of Procyon's drones hopped over the trees.

"Hey, L.T." That would be Detective Stan Bradley, my biggest critic both literally and figuratively. I'd put even odds on him tackling werefox-form Niall in a fight—except, of course, Niall's got those fangs. He caught sight of me and lifted his chin, in a subtle salute I assumed was all the "Hello" I was gonna get.

"Unies canvassed the neighborhood. A couple down the block heard the screaming, either from these poor saps or the monster. No one home to either side. A lot of these homes are part-time residences. No security cameras aimed this way."

"All right. What about its trajectory? Whichever way it went, it had to leave a track."

"What about your consultants?" Bradley pointed at me. "Isn't that their job?"

"I thought it was on your resume now, Bradley." I grinned, which only made his scowl deepen, so, win for me. "SCPD's Extraordinary Crimes Task Force? That's a heck of a thing to stitch onto a logo patch. SCPDECTF. Man. I'd still take one, though, if you're offering."

"I got a good place for you to put it." Bradley shook his head. "I'll broaden the search radius, L.T. Someone has to have seen something."

"Sounds good, Stan." Ramos indicated the hovering drone. "I suspect we'll have some more answers to help us out."

"Yeah, right." Bradley took a step away but stopped. "Hale?"

"What?"

"We nicknamed it the goon squad."

I stared as Bradley headed for the patrol officers hanging around the squad cars. Whatever he said to them wasn't a friendly greeting, because they got super formal with their "sirs" and scattered. "Was he making nice by letting me in on the nickname?"

"He's trying. But this task force has him torn. Stan's a good cop. One of the best in the department. Monsters? Other dimensions? Dark powers? He's having a harder time than I did adjusting."

"I guess I'll take what I can get."

My phone buzzed. Liz. <There's residual tachyons as expected but it'll take me a while to pinpoint a direction of travel and if it's been jumping dimensions in addition to points in this world that'll make extrapolation trickier.>

<Get us as close as you can.>

<Okay yeah sure.>

"What's going on, then? This person is a younger Skipper?" Ramos nudged me.

I'd almost forgotten about my new crew. They weren't gawking. Nope, Bowen was prowling the edges of the scorched earth, hand on his sword's hilt. Niall was crouched opposite us, nose testing the air. He brushed his hand across the grass. "He's from before Skipper visited us, but he absorbed his older self's memories across space and time. How's that for brain-melting?"

"Ah." If it bothered Ramos, he didn't offer any other questions, though I could tell his brain was churning. "Listen. The captain's understandably upset about this, if for no other reason we've gone a decent stretch without these kinds of deaths."

"What, she'd rather we stick to regular murders?"

"She'd rather the task force be gone." Ramos smirked. "Unfortunately for her, the mayor's the one keeping the goon squad afloat. Everyone's seen the videos, Mercury. Astral fiends aren't a secret anymore. I've heard rumors of congressional hearings and feds sniffing around—though after one of Homeland Security's agents turned out to be aiding the enemy, I suspect their investigations are turned more inward that outward."

That struck me like a blade through flesh—and trust me, I knew what that felt like. Serena Cyr. She was Homeland, and yeah, she'd been Alexander Arkwright's lover. Who knew where she was? I could pick out periodic posts off the Internet where she'd been spreading tales about Procyon, but it read like fantasy. "Loredana's still inventorying what all went missing from our Historic Vault."

"More of it gets out, the more there's going to be questions." Ramos rubbed his face. "And when bodies start appearing, panic follows. These three— college students. No bottles, no paraphernalia or residue that's evident, so I'm assuming they weren't here for drugs."

"Extracurricular activities?"

"The flesh is the flesh." Ramos shrugged. "Forensics has their cell phones, what was left of them. If we can pull something from the SIM cards, we might have answers. Our only option for positive ID otherwise is dental records."

My stomach tightened. I went clammy with sweat. Something was wrong with me, that the terribleness of what lay before me didn't strike until now. Meant I was getting use to the horrors. I didn't want that. Not when Loredana and I were planning a life together.

How would that even work? What kind of husband could I be, if I got numb to these deaths?

And what kind of father could I be?

The thought ran me over. Since when had I even considered kids? There were more complex things to deal with before I was ready for anyone to call me, "Dad."

Niall whistled. He was fifty feet from the scorch mark, still crouched, waving at Bowen.

"What's that?" Ramos asked.

"Progress, I hope. Come on."

Bowen reached Niall at the same time. He knelt beside him. "You've found it?"

"The track is faint. Here." Niall encompassed an area of mashed grass inside his hands. Huh. If you squinted, you could see the shape.

"Footprints?" Ramos took a photo with his phone.

"Astral fiend's imprint," I said. "Probably an impact point from one of its tentacles. What'd he do, sniff it out?"

"Niall could track a goblin through the foulest tavern with his eyes closed." Bowen's smile was grim, his expression determined. The guy was ready to hunt. "Show us the way."

Niall nodded. He drew his sword and Bowen did likewise. Before Ramos could issue a warning about bladed weapons, they loped into the woods.

"Uh, L.T.?" That was Bradley. He stood at the sidewalk, his gun drawn.

"Stand down." Ramos sighed, but had his pistol ready. "We'll check it out."

"You want backup?"

I powered up the stave and propped it over my shoulder, yellow-white sparks trailing its wake. Intense cold washed down my arm. "Nah, he's good. Mind the store, Bradley."

Dappled light illuminated the ground inside the tightly packed forest, where the edges of Wells Heights' immaculately trimmed foliage met regular-old nature. Birds chirped high among the leaves, out of sight but flitting from tree to tree. If I blocked out the distant rush of traffic and ignored the lingering odor of burnt grass and flesh, I could have been strolling through the forest outside the city of Meda in my home dimension.

Home. I should contact Teget. If we were going up against a mutated version of an astral fiend, he'd be a prime ally. Who better to help me take down the fire beast than my brother?

But he had his hands full overseeing a fortified temple full of dangerous relics and making sure the Whisperer and his minions didn't launch any more offensives against any dimension.

Ramos and I walked a couple dozen yard behind Bowen and Niall as the two tracked—whatever it was Niall was tracking. The two made the barest noises. I'm sure Ramos and I were more distracting than helpful. Liz's drone was six feet overhead, buzzing like the world's largest but least blood-sucking mosquito.

I stepped on a branch. It snapped.

Bowen whirled. His mouth moved and his palm glowed blazing blue.

"Down!" I slammed into Ramos. We toppled into a patch of pinecones and leaves.

Twin spears of ice, each as big as Ramos' automatic pistol, embedded themselves in a tree. *Thunk, thunk.* They quivered from the impact.

Niall barked a laugh. "And this is why we don't allow stragglers on the hunt."

"My apologies." Bowen offered me a hand.

"Nope. I got it." Didn't want a case of frostbite. I helped Ramos up.

"What did I just see?" Ramos shivered. His breath feathered. It was suddenly cold, like we'd stepped out of a house into a brisk, fall morning.

"It will fade in a moment." Just like the blue glow faded from Bowen's eyes. Creepy.

"He's, um…" I scratched the back of my neck. "Ice magic."

"Summoning," Bowen clarified.

"Yeah. That."

Ramos stared. "But… how?"

"By the power of the gift of the Most High."

"I don't think that's possible." Ramos brushed dirt off his tie. "You and I should have a conversation."

"Guys, if we could postpone the theological debates of sorcery and…" I waved my hand.

"Whatever. Any luck, Niall? Or did we come all this way so your captain could freeze dry my lieutenant?"

Niall snorted. "Luck, my tail. Scent and skill, whelp."

He held up a stick that was as long as my forearm. Badly twisted, black and purple, but still a—

Wait a second. It dripped thick, blue ooze that was nearly black. Violet sparks trickled from knobby bark.

Not bark. Hide.

"It's a piece of the astral fury," I murmured.

"I thought they sublimated when they were cut off," Ramos said.

I took the ruined tentacle from Niall and held it up so Liz's drone could get a good look. "They do. But whatever this thing is, we better make sure it's not dropping more pieces of itself, because the last time that happened, we had a zombie plague on our hands."

CHAPTER EIGHT

I wanted to get the nasty thing back to the Procyon lab ASAP, but Ramos and Loredana overruled me. Ramos ranted about disturbing a crime scene, while Loredana was worried we might lose whatever tenuous connection the piece of astral fury might have to its surroundings. She didn't want to risk our tracking efforts.

So, she brought Tracking into the woods.

Liz prowled around the tentacle. She had it stuffed inside a clear container. The way she looked at it suggested a cat watching a fishbowl—except this fish was already dead and was technically only a ruined fin.

The tentacle sat in a clear, fizzing solution of—something. Liz had listed the chemical compounds but all I got out of it was that the stuff preserved the limb. A quartet of white boxes surrounded the container, each one trailing gray and blue wires that snaked into the liquid.

"It should have sublimated, even in the solution." Liz peered so close to the container her breath feathered the cool, transparent acrylic. "But it didn't."

"No kidding." I leaned against the tree that Bowen had impaled with icicles. They dripped steadily as they melted in the warming weather. A broken branch dug into my spine. Didn't make me move. Whatever we were dealing with was an anomaly. I hated the thought. Give me monsters that evaporated once I'd slain them.

"Does the dual nature of the creature have any bearing?" Loredana stood a foot from the box, her arms folded. She was dressed like she was on her way to a board meeting, all business and elegance, but she glared at the piece of astral fury like its existence was a personal affront. "It's tethered to both this dimension and the other."

"Could be." Liz consulted a tablet screen. Didn't take off her shades to read the indecipherable glowing symbols mixed with regular old letters and numbers. "There's definitely waves of dimensional distortion, similar to what we see when rips open and close, but there's aspects too that are like when Gemini triggers his portals. So, it's simultaneously drawing its existence from the Interstice like astral fiends do but it also bypassing the typical transit methods."

Gemini. Dominic Zein. The guy who could not only teleport from Point A to Point B on Earth, but through the Interstice—safely—to my home dimension of Meda. Oh, and he captured his evil twin from an alternate version of Earth, thus preventing a pandemic or something. Nice guy. A little bossy, but then again, I was surrounded by a lot of people with that trait.

I tapped my phone against my belt. His number was right there. Who better to help me chase down a hard-to-find monster that so far was eluding our best Tracking gimmicks?

But the guy had a life. And a wife. Someone who he loved dearly and, I'd guess would be hesitant to be away from to put himself in more danger.

I glanced at Loredana. Heat burned my cheeks. Speaking of married, I was gonna be the same guy soon.

"If we're done brining or pickling or whatever you're doing to that rubbish," Niall muttered, "I'd best be on the prowl for our adversary."

"Easy, Fido." I said. "Let Liz pinpoint the guy before we go rampaging across the city."

"We could have been doing just that, rather than standing about as if waiting for fair maidens to serve us meat and mead. I'll not lounge while I could be scouring the streets for the fiend!"

"I for one would rather narrow the search." Ramos had his hands on his hips. The sun glinted off his SCPD badge. "And before anyone gets any ideas about 'prowling,' let me remind you that neither of you men are affiliated with Procyon Foundation. You're sure not authorized by our task force."

"Peasant soldiers?" Niall sniffed. "I think not.

This is the realm of sorcery, constable, and I'll thank you to leave the real warriors to it."

Ramos took a step toward the red-headed man with the sword—same guy who could turn into a fanged werefox—before Bowen shot a wall of ice between them.

"Wow. Oh, wow." Liz lifted her sunglasses but immediately winced and put them back into place.

"Confound it all, Niall!" Bowen snapped. "This constable of the law is a servant of the Most High, and you would quarrel with him? We are the strangers in this land. We would heed his counsel if we are to succeed in our quest."

"This again." Niall sighed. "What would you have me do? Gaze into the lady's magical glass and twiddle my thumbs until she gives me a command?"

"Well, you don't have to wait around—I mean, by yourself." Liz stood quickly. She bumped the container with her shoe, setting the suspension liquid sloshing. The fizzing intensified, obscuring the tentacle fragment behind bubbles. "So, I mean, I could take you to some of the possible locations to investigate. Not that I brought my car. I didn't. Garvey drove but he's a really good driver and—"

Niall smiled. "It is not that I would not find the company pleasant, but the sooner I can end my hunt in this strange dreamland, the sooner I can get Bowen back to our ship and home to our isle."

"It's not a dream." Liz's voice barely rose over a whisper. "Why would you say that?"

"Because the real world has angels in it." Niall's sword was jabbed into the dirt by his leg. He wrested it free, swiped dirt from the blade across his sleeve, and stowed it in his scabbard. He gave the ice wall a shove. It was only a couple inches thick, so it toppled.

Ramos stepped back, letting the ice shards crumble around him. Niall brushed past. Ramos' hand snapped around his bicep. "If I hear reports of you messing around in my city, I don't care what your 'magic' is—I'll lock you up so fast you'll get your tail caught between the bars. *Comprende?*"

Niall snarled and broke free. He stormed toward the neighborhood.

Liz sank down beside the container. I knelt next to her and put a hand on her shoulder. That Niall. What a tool.

"I apologize for his behavior," Bowen said. "Niall's temper is as untamed as a cyclone. Were he not more kin to me than a brother of my own blood, we could have very well dueled to our demises years ago."

"I get that he's impatient," I said. "But he'd better grow up. We're not gonna get anything done by running off without a plan, one at a time. This is a team. No room for solo acts. The sooner you two get that, the better."

"I understand, Mercury, but keep in mind, he is also my crew. Thus, he looks to me for orders—and I have none with which to satisfy him."

Ramos chuckled.

"What?" I asked.

"Not a thing, sir." He smiled and donned his sunglasses. "Come on, Captain Cord. I had better make sure my people don't handcuff your friend to the nearest squad car."

Once they were gone, Liz sucked in a breath. She stood, rubbing at the corners of her eyes, which were still hidden by the shades. "Okay. So, I've got Cyril running extrapolations on the astral fury's appearances, and with the data we get from the dimensional distortions enveloping this piece, we shouldn't have any trouble figuring out where the astral fury is."

I gave her shoulder a squeeze. "Nice work. I'll distract our wayward magicians in the meantime. How about it, Loredana? Pizza at Carlito's?"

She blushed. I mean, full on red cheeks. This is the lady who emptied an automatic weapon at zombies and astral fiends in the middle of a torrential downpour. "Sadly, I have a Chamber of Commerce luncheon to attend. Procyon's public arm must continue to support community initiatives if we're to maintain at least a semblance of secrecy about what we really do."

"Fair enough."

"But." She kissed my cheek. "Do be a lamb and bring me mozzarella sticks."

"Yes, ma'am."

I helped Liz gather up the devices scattered around the tentacle, stowing them into a bag that reminded me of the kind used to carry a slow cooker, then lifted the box itself. "Hey, you said you rode here with Garvey. Did he bring his van?"

"Procyon Security?" Liz wrinkled her nose. "Yeah. It smells like boy."

"Perfect." I grinned. "I've got an idea to cheer up Niall."

Ramos shook his head.

"Oh, come on. It's ideal!" I spread my arms.

"No. Absolutely not."

"Ramos," I groaned. "Don't be such a baby."

"We don't know anything about him! He could kill people!"

"Could, but won't, because of Bowen his captain." Ramos scowled.

"Look, the guy is a warrior from another planet and for all we know, another time period. He's a great asset! And plus, I broke his gun."

"So take him to a sporting goods store! Or Wal-Mart! *Dios mio*, Mercury, there's background checks and rules for a reason! Too many people are trigger happy without adding a volatile alien vigilante to the mix."

"I'm not asking you for permission, you realize."

"But you're asking my blessing. I won't give it."

"Fine." I rolled my eyes. "I'll get Loredana to hire him for Procyon Security. Then this conversation will continue with her. But I need all the help I can get on this one, Ramos, and short of calling in the superhero gang…"

"You should, you know. Call them."

"We're not quite at crisis level, yet. It's one monster." I pointed at the open door of the Procyon van. "And we're about to add our own."

Garvey, one of the Procyon Security veterans, was describing his inventory to Niall. Did I say inventory? I should call it, armory. MP5 machine guns. Beretta semi-automatics. Shotguns and rifles and an assortment of pistols. Garvey himself was best described as a weapon, albeit a thick-bodied brawler with a beard that he'd grown out over the past few months. Brown hair swept the edge of his collar. His buzzcut hadn't gotten any longer.

Niall stared into the van, mouth agape. The guy who spoke of angels looked like he'd seen one.

"Oh, hey, Mr. Hale." Garvey nodded. "I'm showing Mr. … Phelan, right? Mr. Phelan what's available. He seems partial to the FN."

The FN being a SCAR battle rifle. Niall turned it over in his hands. "And—the ramrod?"

"No need." Garvey went through the drill of loading, aiming, emptying, the whole nine yards. Niall accepted it back. He held it at his shoulder, like he was born to shoot it.

"I cannot believe this exists," Niall murmured. "And here I fawned over a well-oiled wheellock mechanism."

"If you're good, sir, I got these ready for him."

Garvey passed Bowen a black duffel bag. From the way Bowen shouldered it I gathered it weighed a ton. "Couple of pistols, easily concealed under their clothes—holsters, extra mags. The works."

"What, no Procyon Security shirts?" I asked.

"Two ballcaps." Garvey gave me a crooked smile. "Didn't have their sizes."

"My man." I squinted into the dark recesses of the van at a bulky device that looked like a radar gun and a floodlight had a child. "You've got the portal gun out for a spin?"

"It was under review by some Procyon techs from the Chicago office. They took a liking to it, but Liz wanted it back pronto." Garvey shrugged. "Says she's got a brainstorm."

"Those are usually awesome."

Niall and Bowen armed themselves with pistols. Niall slung the rifle by its strap. I gestured at the bag. "Better stow it for now. It's, uh, frowned upon to walk around in daylight with that puppy on a leash."

"I'll not let this out of my sight," Niall said. "Never."

"You think that's great?" I clapped him on the shoulder. "Wait until you taste pizza."

Twenty-Second and DeLeon. My home away from home. Okay, second home, I guess, if you counted Procyon. My shoes squeaked on white tile floors. I ran a hand over the olive-green paint on the walls.

Niall inspected the black and white photos of celebrities. "These are warriors of great fame?"

I chuckled. "Suppose you could call Stallone that, yeah. Let's get a table. You guys need a pie."

Twenty minutes later, we had a gorgeous pepperoni and sausage pizza casting steam from the center of a four-top. Bowen ate his slice with the slowest chews. I swore time itself had failed. And Niall? He wouldn't stop grinning, even with cheese trapped between his teeth.

"We're truly indebted to your hospitality, Mercury." I was impressed Bowen waited until his mouth wasn't bulging with his last bite. "I wish we could return that favor."

"I don't make a habit of playing tourist on other worlds."

"But the physician—he said this is not your home, did he not?"

A big white metro bus flashed by the window. I gazed at the traffic, the crowds on the sidewalk, the bike messengers zipping between everyone, even the homeless guy pushing his shopping cart full of cans and cardboard. Seagulls. Sirens. Kids swearing. Music blaring from a low-rider. Old ladies laughing at a joke as they passed us.

"He's right. Sort off." I snagged a pepperoni round off a pizza slice. "I wasn't born here, not even in this world, let alone this city. But San Camillo's where I grew up. It's where I learned everything I needed to know. It's where I found friends—family. And when I discovered where I really came from, it just expanded the definition, you know? Of home. Those chances I've gotten to go to Meda, I walk stone streets and think, 'I'm home.' Then I come back through a portal to San Camillo and smell garbage stinking in the heat and the hot dog water and the bay breeze... It's the same feeling. I'm in both places."

Bowen nodded, a smile broadening on his face. "There is an isle I call home. Yet I cannot deny the joy it brings when I set foot on the deck of *Northwind*, riding the currents that carry us across the Atlan. A man can give pieces of his heart to more than one land, so that he finds comfort wherever he may be. Yet, that is not all that comforts the soul."

"This is when he would start in the sermon." Niall dragged cheese off his slice with his teeth. He belched and wiped his mouth with the back of his hand. "Let me be the one to rescue you."

"Thanks." I chuckled. "Appreciate your guy's help on this."

"Not a great deal of choice in the matter, but Bowen seems to trust you." Niall slurped his glass of beer. Then he sneezed. "That accursed foam. Mind, I cannot fathom how it's possible he remembers being in this dreamland without it having happened yet, but I'm not one to dwell on the philosopher's questions. I need only a target and a weapon to discharge."

"Got that fixed up for you, didn't I?"

"You did." Niall sneered. "Yet you still owe me a pouch of silver for the ruined musket."

That got a good laugh from Bowen and me. Not a bad way to spend an afternoon—pizza, beers, good (but strange) company.

So of course, that's when the people on the street started screaming.

My phone rattled across the table, clattering to the floor before I could catch it. In the few seconds it took to duck underneath and return with it, a car slid down the street upside down, its chassis burning.

"Well now," Bowen murmured. "I would say your hunt has been curtailed, Niall."

The astral fury squeezed between the buildings on Twenty-Second. Tentacles—including one that was truncated—slashed at the offices on either side, shattering glass. People scattered in all directions.

Squeezed? Yeah. It was forty feet tall. When had it been taking evil monster steroids?

"What's our strategy?" Niall snapped.

"Get to the car and get your weapons." I reached down by the seat and retrieved a backpack. Liz and Loredana made sure I'd left Procyon with it in my car, especially since I didn't have it during my last daylight brawl with the astral fury.

It didn't hurt that the suit amplified my powers.

I unzipped the backpack on my run toward the back of Carlito's. Nobody stopped me, because the customers and employees fled out the doors to the street and the alley like rats off a sinking ship.

"Whelp!" Niall had his hand on the door. "Where are you headed?"

"To the can!" I snapped. "Where else am I gonna put on my superhero suit?"

CHAPTER NINE

Thirty-eight seconds.

That's how long it took me to slip into the suit. Not too shabby. And not too hard, really, considering it was a glorified jumpsuit that adhered to my body.

No idea how Airfoil got himself into armor and a helmet that fast. But I digress.

I burst out the front door into a cacophony of screams, sirens, and screeching brakes. Cars backed up along Twenty-Second caused one heck of a traffic jam. People abandoned vehicles left, right, and center, meaning anyone who had the sense to try to turn around found himself blocked in and had to abandon ship also.

The astral fury didn't seem to mind, because it lashed out at the commingled cars instead of people. Man. Everyone parked there was gonna have a terrible time dealing with insurance adjustors—and whatever guy they sent out to assess damage would be scratching his head the whole time. It didn't mean the area was devoid of people. Pockets of scared drivers-turned-pedestrians huddled in store entryways and behind a city bus left unattended.

Had to get them out of the way first.

I drew as much power as I could from the pulsar stave, even as the suit's crazy circuitry siphoned some of it off. The more it took, the better the suit camouflaged me against the urban setting. Plus, it stored more for me to draw back, like a capacitor I could access if I happened to drop the stave. Which, it should be noted, was a bad idea.

It didn't seem like I needed the stealth, though, because Bowen and Niall were providing a doozy of a distraction. Niall sprinted toward the cars, stepped up the bumper and then the hood of a limousine, and dragged himself onto the roof. He leveled the rifle. Guy knew how to hold a modern gun, that was for sure.

"You!" he howled. "Foul beast! I'll strip your stinking hide and use it for sails!"

The SCAR opened up, a harsh rattling, as Niall let the astral fury have what must have been an entire magazine. However hot the monster was, the temperature didn't melt bullets, because it reeled as gunfire ripped chunks of hide from its limbs.

Shrieks pounded the air. I'm pretty sure a pair of windows blew out in response, on either side of the street. I was still a couple hundred yards off, but I was near enough the heat put off by the ugly thing washed over me like I was standing in a jet engine's exhaust.

My earbud emitted a burst of static. "I've seen it on the news." Loredana's voice could have been announcing a slight drizzle forecast for the afternoon. "You have to get it out of downtown."

"Thanks, I guessed that part." I dodged sideways as a tentacle slapped down from the sky. My jump took me a full story toward a window full of hairdressers and their customers. Apparently whatever style they were working on was too vital for them to escape impending death. I hit the window hard enough to leave cracks beneath my feet and pushed off, hurtling toward the monster.

Who, it should be said, was gigantic.

Right. Forty feet. Even though he seemed to lack the better regenerative properties he'd had when he was smaller, his attitude was just as foul—as if he knew he was the biggest, baddest thing on the block.

I realized like the big idiot I was that I was arrowing right for his hide—which was completely ablaze.

A torrent of freezing wind battered me aside, as a storm of sleet in broad daylight extinguished a patch of the astral fury's backside that was large enough for a guy like me to land on. Bowen was on the trunk of the limo, pouring wave after wave of icy streams at the fiend. He seemed to be concentrating on its limbs, dousing fires at the lashing tentacles. I didn't see any offices or stores burning, but there was plenty of smoke turning the block into a hazy nightmare.

I landed, using the pulsar stave as an anchor—which, you know, the astral fiend didn't appreciate because doing so meant stabbing deep through its skin. Tentacles flung around, trying to separate me from its hindquarters, like I was the world's worst mosquito bite. Bonus: The creature couldn't see me, thanks to the suit's adaptive camouflage rendering me the same blackened mush as the astral fury's hide.

I separated the stave's halves and used the part not keeping me from falling way too far to the pavement as a defensive weapon. Come to think of it, the pavement was a ways down there. I could see the writhing shadow.

It was shrinking.

"Loredana?" I hollered. "If this thing can fly, now's a really good time to tell me."

"It does appear to be ascending."

"Well, someone better tell it I didn't sign up for a hot-air balloon ride! Any bright ideas? This is gonna take longer than the average astral fiend takedown!"

"A moment." The overlapping voices in the background reminded me of a crowded concert hall waiting for the conductor's baton to rise. "I have word from Lieutenant Ramos that SCPD's special task force should be able to help interdict. Stand by."

"Standing by is about what I'm *not* going to do." I ripped the embedded half of the stave free and jumped the length of two cars along the hide, toward the cluster of blazing eyes. Shrieks and screams assailed me; no earbud could block out the sound.

Below, the streams of ice shifted direction. Bowen was prowling the edges of the shadow, shooting shards and coating hide wherever I wasn't. Best guess? He was trying to make the astral fury take damage from more than one angle, in hopes of confusing it.

Niall lent a hand with his constant taunts and gunfire.

The astral fury lost patience with him first. It dropped back to the pavement at a startling speed, throwing up chunks of asphalt. I would have been bucked off if I hadn't wrapped my arms around a tentacle, well clear of the spikes that would like nothing more than to drain the life from every cell of my body.

Niall clicked through the last round of his gun— what had that been, three, four magazines?—and drew his sword. "Come on, then! Give me something into which to sink my fangs!"

His T-shirt shredded as his form bulged, red and white fur erupting, fangs protruding. The astral fury's tentacle smashed toward him and he swept his katana up, intercepting the blow. The blade sliced deep, cutting down the middle like you'd split a carrot in two, then got itself wedged.

The astral fury turned toward Niall, fangs protruding and screams filling the air.

Niall howled in response. The claws on his feet— so much for those boots, too—dug into the asphalt as the monster pushed down on him.

That's when I reached its eyes.

I drove the halves of the stave deep into one eye apiece and drew on as much of the power stashed in the suit as I could. That made me visible, but hey, all I looked like was a mishmash of gray and black slashes, stripes, and polygons.

Bowen sent a barricade of ice crunching through the street, eight feet tall and with a leading edge that must have been sharp as Niall's sword because it cut a pickup truck neatly in two from its grill to gate before severing the tentacle Niall was engaged with.

And speaking of cutting, a new sound sliced across the monster's caterwauling. A heavy, droning beat. Propeller blades. A helicopter?

It was one of those military types, a Blackhawk, that pounced over the tops of the buildings like a hunchbacked dragonfly. It was painted black and white instead of standard dull gray.

I spotted a gleaming SCPD emblem on one door before said door flew open and a barrage of bullets rained down on the astral fury.

At the same time, S.W.A.T. teams of officers clad in all black fatigues and armor swarmed from multiple alleys around the blocks. Four guys each, armed with automatic rifles. The lead officer of each contingent had a thick tube under the gun's barrel. Those triggered with a muffled *whump* and puff of smoke.

Explosions battered the astral fury from all sides.

Grenade launchers? Chopper-mounted machine guns? Ramos wasn't kidding about upgrades to his goon squad. That is, the SCPDECTF. Yeah, goon squad's easier on the brain.

I was hanging on for dear life, trying not to get bucked off.

Niall was clawing at a rampaging tentacle as Bowen iced it down, turning the flaming hide into a hissing, shriveled parody of itself.

All in all, way better than the last fight.

That is, until the sky opened.

The portal formed without warning—nothing from Loredana or Liz or anyone else at Procyon. One minute, sunny blue sky wreathed in smoke. The next, a black hole rimmed with purple, like someone had unzipped the atmosphere clear to space.

Another astral fury emerged from it.

Not another. I mean, it looked like a massive spider, bristling with hair and fire, but the similarities strengthened the nearer it got to its counterpart—until they merged in a thunderclap.

A massive surge of energy rippled across its skin, a warped, perverted version of the golden-white that the pulsar stave emitted.

I shoved off and somersaulted down to the street.

Should've managed a graceful landing on the nearest car, but the leg buckled as I hit, so I rolled down the windshield onto the hood. I was too flabbergasted by what I was seeing to be mad about its umpteenth glitch.

The astral fury was good as new.

Gone was the gaping maw, and the damaged,

severed tentacles. It looked like a giant, hulking brain, trailing more tendrils than I could count, its pulsating, bulging body draped with gleaming eyespots. It would have been pitch black but for the eerie, violet and orange flames streaming in the crevasses and folds. The adjoining buildings crunched from the strain as it expanded, gaining another twenty feet all around.

"It can't be." One of the S.W.A.T. leaders who'd led the grenade assault removed his face mask. Ramos. Sweat beaded his eyebrows. He made the sign of the cross. "It's unstoppable."

"Nothing's unstoppable," I growled. "You guys ready?"

Bowen held on to Niall's shoulder. Poor guy looked like he'd been standing in the middle of the Antarctic for a couple days—skin as pale as the marble coating the bank down the street, purple under his eyes like he'd fought in a boxing match. "Give me—a spell in which to gather my strength."

Niall's fur was matted in a couple places on his sides and there was a pink stain on his chest. Blood dripped down one leg. "What did the man Garvey call them?" he snapped. "Magazines? I require a dozen and a half more."

Their fighting spirit aside, I had no idea how to tackle this guy. It was as if someone playing a massive video game had hit "Reset" and we didn't have any extra lives for this boss battle. Even the cops up in the helicopter must have had second thoughts, because they wheeled away, putting distance between themselves and the astral fury.

At least the thing's pause gave time for people to stream out of the damaged buildings.

"Get them out of the block!" Ramos hollered at his officers. "Take every civilian out of the perimeter!"

"Mercury," Loredana said. "Liz informs me that the temporary portal merged our dimension with another whose temporal signature matches that of the readings she obtained the night our two travelers emerged."

"So that was the mutated arachnafury." I gasped, digging deep for a breath. The pulsar stave's power was draining from my body. As a result, I was less super-me and more tired-beat-up-me. "The one from Bowen's realm... Came in here? Joined with itself?"

"They were already paired. This is a solidification, so there is no longer a separation between itself."

That made my head spin. Or maybe it was a concussion. "We need major backup."

"Wilhelmina is on her way with a contingent of Procyon Security, led by Garvey."

"The portal gun?"

"Disassembled and with Elizabeth's hands deep in its inmost parts."

"Of course." I blew out a breath. I rejoined the pulsar stave and spun it once. "Send a message to Dom... er, Gemini. We're gonna need his help on this one. See if he can teleport Airfoil to us."

"Understood." Loredana paused. "Mercury, we're reading a spike in tachyon—"

The signal cut out in a screech of static and feedback. The astral fury quivered, letting off a horrific moan that dug deep inside my head. The temperature on the entire block must have spiked twenty degrees. Fleeing civilians dropped a handful at a time, overcome by the moans or the heat or both.

Bowen fell to his hands and knees. I thought he was gonna throw up.

"Steady on." Niall crouched with him. "Do not succumb. I'll not have to drag your carcass off these accursed avenues."

"It's—there's so much pain." Bowen clutched the sides of his head. "Most High, make this cease!"

Tentacles snapped out like whips. One, three, five—it took eleven people in its grasp, drawing them upward.

Of all the luck... I punched Ramos in the shoulder. "If you got snipers, cut them loose!"

I jumped as far and fast as I could, toward the nearest huddle of captured people, ignoring Ramos' warning shouts. A quick swipe cut three of them free, and I tackled them—an old Pakistani man, a teen Latina, and a middle-aged white guy. We were low enough I let them fall, screaming, onto the awnings along storefronts that hadn't burned down.

But I wasn't fast enough. Ramos' snipers were equally ineffective. Their shots punched through tentacles but didn't sever them. Even though I got two more free, the other six had their life drained so quickly their bodies shriveled and went blotchy gray. They were instantly mummified. The astral fury drew the desiccated corpses into its underside, where each one dissolved in a shimmering, black-speckled purple mist.

I slammed into the top of an SUV so hard I dented the roof. Pain lanced up my wounded leg clear into my hip. Really hoped I hadn't shattered it.

The astral fury spun around and blasted free of downtown. The helicopter spun wildly in its wake—until it fell, the rotors bent beyond use.

No more deaths on my watch.

Nice idea, but I couldn't move. The pain kept me anchored to the SUV, even with the pulsar stave feeding me enough energy to set every cell vibrating. I watched, horror bringing me close to tears, as the chopper spiraled. It was toast.

Bowen managed an ice blast that caught the underside, slowing but not stopping the fall. Went it was within thirty feet of the ground, Niall braced himself. He grabbed the underside, roaring as he was shoved through abandoned cars.

The chopper slammed to a halt against a bus, Niall buried beneath the wreck.

I saw Bowen slump against a flattened cab and watched Ramos drag Niall from under a car door right before I threw up.

CHAPTER TEN

Have to say, I was getting real sick of losing to that overgrown jellyfish.

Procyon's security gang got us bundled up and whisked out of downtown within seconds of Garvey screeching up in his van, followed by two silver SUVs. Wilhelmina was there, too, but didn't do much except hold my hand as we bounced over the roads toward the silo base.

She didn't need to say anything. We blew it. Again. And we were way more prepared than during that first group face-off in the woods.

What was I supposed to do against an astral fiend that had merged with a monster from another dimension, then absorbed that alternate self, and kept growing ginormous?

Plus, it was getting antsy.

I stood in Tracking with arms folded. Aerial news footage broadcast from one of San Camillo's big networks showed an ugly black line tracing its way into the hills. Firefighters hustled families from their homes as the blaze spread down Arbor Valley, threatening more homes that your typical wildfire. The astral fury burnt so much acreage in a short time it created a permanent pillar of smoke that blocked out attempts to pinpoint its location.

"Si. I understand. We've got it, sir." Ramos ended his call. His face still glistened with sweat. Probably because he was still geared up in S.W.A.T. fatigues and armor. "Air National Guard is coordinating with the forest service. They're debating whether they should hold off the slurry bombers fighting the fires so the military can send in the real thing loaded down with enough high explosive to turn the hills into a second lunar landscape."

"Let me guess: No one can make a decision." My heart thudded under my ribcage. I was so mad I couldn't put much more of a quip together. It felt like my arms were the only thing keeping my chest from exploding. "No one can figure out what to do about this monster."

"It's more the debate about whether the solution will inflict more damage than the problem." Ramos attempted to smooth his hair. A tuft refused to be tamed. "If you haven't already called for your kind of backup, now would be the time."

"First two calls went to voicemail." I mashed my finger on the speed dial icon on my phone. "Here goes number three."

Voicemail. What kind of superhero doesn't check

his messages? Or texts? Each one I sent steadily approached Rated R in terms of verbiage.

This time the phone clicked. "Hey, quit calling."

I scowled. "Who is this?"

"This is the guy who's not gonna let you talk to Airfoil." The voice dripped with condescension, but not the kind you'd pick up from someone who thought he was a brainiac. No, this was way too smarmy to be an adult. Plus, it cracked on the word "not."

Teenager.

"Listen, kid, this is Mercury Hale. Brandon knows all about me and I know all about him. So, do me a favor? Go get your dad."

"He's gone."

"Gone where?"

"If I knew the *where*, I'd have said *where*." He sighed so loudly into the receiver it blew static. "What do you want?"

"What do I want? Have you seen the news from San Camillo? I want your dad to fly through a portal I'll happily provide so he can mash our latest monster flat with his gravity powers!"

"He'd do it, too, but like, he's not here. I don't know where he is. Secret mission, I guess."

"And he left his kid home alone?"

"His *partner*." The teen snapped out the last work. "I get it. You got big problems. But so does he. If he gets back in time to help, I'll tell him. Otherwise, quit bugging me. I've got homework."

"Wait a second, you—"

The call dropped.

My mouth kept working but no words exited.

"Problem?" Ramos asked.

"Yeah. I just got hung up on by a 15-year-old sidekick." I slammed my phone down on the table.

"Take it easy. Bashing useful things isn't going to help anything. You'll need to be calm and focused to figure out how to destroy this creature."

"Calm and focused? I'm 0-3 with the astral fury, Ramos. I'm past rational thinking."

"Which would be a mistake, because if you truly are, then you won't be able to save anyone." He prodded my chest with a finger. "Including you. And if you're dead, we're all doomed."

I clenched my teeth. He was right. I hated it, but he was right. This was no time to explode. I had to do something, and if I was preoccupied rampaging through Procyon's secret base, that meant zero time spent planning. I exhaled. Suddenly all the adrenaline tanked. I slumped into a chair.

"Better?" Ramos sat opposite me.

"I think so. It'll take me a bit." I shook my head. "Did you seriously use 'doomed' in a sentence?"

"I thought it would get your attention." He smiled.

Loredana and Wilhelmina came in, heads ducked as they whispered a conversation. Loredana hurried nearer as soon as she realized I was there and knelt by my side. "You really must let Doctor Becker examine your wounds."

"Bumps and bruises, all of which are healing fast. Nothing broken. Ramos checked."

"As much as I trust the lieutenant, I would prefer the opinion of a medical professional." She cocked her head, like she was examining me for those same injuries, but I figured she was trying to look deeper. "What of Airfoil?"

"Zilch. He's AWOL and his brat kid won't tell us where—if he even knows."

"Then Gemini could be our best bet."

"I'll message him again." I shook my head. "Superheroes. Worse than customer service when you're trying to get help on the phone."

"Bowen and Niall are still recuperating in the in-firmary." Loredana stood. "As for Manager Alvarez, well, I suppose I should admit him for observation, given the spike in his blood pressure."

"It could have been a lot worse."

"I'm acknowledging that. Keep in mind, though, that several people died in full view of police armed with heavy weaponry and public armed with cell phones taking video. The federal government has expressed its thanks to Procyon for intervening, even if it cannot be mentioned in public."

"Not that people aren't talking," Ramos said. "There's been a flood of calls to SCPD and the mayor's office, everyone wondering what Procyon and Mercury are going to do to stop the monster."

Them and me both. I rubbed my face. Could've

slept for the next ten years. "Okay, recap. Bowen and Niall are injured. I'm fair to middling. SCPD lost their chopper, which would be handy, and the Air National Guard's still drawing straws as to whether they get to napalm downtown San Camillo. The superhero with the ability to smash this mutated monster like a fly on our windshield is missing in action, and our portal-hopper isn't answering his phone. That sum things up?"

"Quite." Loredana arched an eyebrow. "I would add to that list Elizabeth's locking herself away in one of the makeshift laboratories with the portal gun designed by Mister DeBarthe. Apparently, she has had a brainstorm of cyclonic proportions."

Gary DeBarthe. Another person who died because of me, who I should have been able to save. That list was getting way too long and too heavy to carry. "Let me know when she saves the day."

"Hey." Ramos caught up with me as I brushed by them on my way to the door. His voice was a harsh whisper. "Remember what I said? These people need you. Especially Loredana, whether she shows it or not. You're not going to be able to walk out on her whenever the mood suits, Mercury. The two of you will be bound for good."

"Tell that to the city municipal courts."

Ramos balled his fists. No joke. I've seen the guy mad, but never thought he was gonna take a swing at me. But I deserved it. Stupid comment. I was hurting, both inside and out, and chose to lash around me for easy targets like I was a pain-crazed astral fiend.

"Sorry. I know what you meant. And I believe it."

"You'd better. Or there's more than just your city that's doomed." He turned back to the monitor and made a phone call.

"And on that cheery note…" I headed deeper into the base.

"Hey!" Wilhelmina broke her silence. "Where you think you're off to in a huff?"

"Anywhere but Tracking," I muttered.

Liz was in the lab. Where Procyon's had been the tidiest of spaces, scrubbed free of any possible contaminants, this space was a cold, bare set of concrete walls and slab. A straight-up box. Wires ran in thick bundles across the ceiling and walls, like highways of electricity and data. A row of bright white lab coats hung by the door.

"Mercury!" Liz waved from the middle of the cavernous compartment. Like I needed the indication of where she was. That pink hair could have been a set of fireworks over San Camillo Bay on the Fourth. "Oh, good! I was hoping you'd come by but I was all set to text you so you could start the demonstration."

"Doesn't inspire much confidence when you need my help, Liz." Whatever she was working on was obscured by tall metal boxes and a couple of tarps with holes chewed in the sides. "Loredana said you were working on the portal gun."

"Portal gun?"

"Yeah. Clunky, handheld thing, looks like a radar device that's eaten a power-up mushroom?"

She giggled. "It's not like Super Mario, silly. We totally rebuilt it! I mean, not totally, because the core components remain the same and while I've managed to narrow the confinement stream and drop the temperature way, way down—"

I cleared my throat and indicated my watch.

"Yeesh. Somebody's grumpy." She gave me a hug, squeezing her arms around my middle so hard I thought my spleen would pop out of—wherever a spleen lives, internally speaking. Then she poked her fingers into the corner of my frown until she'd forced it upward. Not a smile, but maybe a grimace doing its best impersonation of one. "Better! We'll work on it."

"I'd rather work on your new toy."

"Oh, you don't have to work on it." Her smile outshone anyone else's I'd encountered all day. "You get to play."

She swung the tarp away, and I gotta admit, I gasped. Not quite "Squee!" but close.

The new device was a dark rectangle carved with readout screens and indicators. There were labels at various points for things like "WARNING: ELECTROCUTION HAZARD," AND "CAUTION: HEAT SINK." The thing had to be four feet long.

"Wow," I said.

"Come on, you haven't even tried it yet!" She tapped my thigh, her fingers clinking where the pulsar stave was hidden in a holster.

I drew the stave, letting it gain power. It cast a warm glow in the sickly-lit lab. "I take it I need this?"

"That's your power source." She pointed to a slot under the grip, behind the trigger.

I plugged it in. The yellow-white energy seeped up into the weapon. A low hum built, filling the room with a subtle vibration that set my teeth buzzing. Blue light spread along sharp angles throughout the device, until the muzzle end started—steaming.

"What'd you make, a giant teapot?"

She rolled her eyes, still grinning. "Pick it up!"

I did. Ice cold. I suppressed shivers. Yeah, that wasn't steam at the far end. It was mist.

"It siphons the tachyon energy from the pulsar stave the way your suit and your leg do, but it converts them into an extreme cold. Narang found a prototype in storage. I don't know what Winston had in mind for it—maybe to immobilize astral fiends instead of destroying them?"

Winston Yen. The former head of Tracking and local tech genius, who, as it turned out, helped his wife open a stable gateway to the Interstice so astral fiends could flood our dimension. Now Marigold was gone, merged with the Whisperer and Arkwright, and her hubby was locked up in a state prison.

Since he also designed my power-absorbing, adaptive camouflage supersuit, I guessed I couldn't fuss too much.

I hefted the gun. It was surprisingly well-balanced,

for as long as it was. "Any particular target?"

Liz pointed at the opposite end of the room, where a stack of three cardboard boxes tottered against the damp concrete wall. She crossed her fingers.

"Yippie kay-yay." I aimed and squeezed the trigger.

The beam was brilliant blue, laced with white bolts of energy, dripping—I don't know, excess tachyons?—along the floor. It struck the boxes. They shattered into thousands of tiny shards that blasted like snow in a blizzard. I shielded my face with the gun.

Liz finally peeked over her fingers. Her hair and eyebrows were frosted white.

"I think," I said slowly, "I'm going to like this."

The rest of the gang was waiting in Tracking. Bowen was there, sporting new bruises and still as pale as a guy recovering from the flu. I sidled up to Loredana. "Everything okay?"

"Are you addressing the rest of us, or myself?" She regarded me with a manner a couple of degrees cooler than the ice-weapon I just tested.

"I'm sorry about earlier. This astral fury—and the leg..." I shook my head. "Nothing's gonna get better if I shut everyone out every time things get rough. So, if you can bear with me, I'll keep pushing through."

She took my hand. "Good. Because we need you here, to take command."

"I'm ready." I winked. "First thing I gotta do, of course, is get Saito-on-Sky booked."

"Perhaps that should wait until directly after we avert fiery destruction." Her smile was sly.

"I can do that. How about we start by finding another way to get out into the forest and as close to the astral fury as we can?" I pointed in the general direction of the garage. "Because there's no way I'm risking my car again."

Ramos cleared his throat. "I don't think anyone wants to drive up into those hills, not as torn up as those roads can be."

"Would that I could command *Northwind* in this realm, we could sail the clouds to our destination," Bowen said.

An air raid? I'd heard worse plans. "Which wouldn't be a bad idea, because I'm guessing SCPD won't drag out another helo after the first one belly-flopped on Twenty-Second."

Ramos frowned. "We're fresh out of military surplus. I could see if my contacts in the Air National Guard would grant us special dispensation."

Loredana held up her hands. "That won't be necessary, any of you. Come with me."

We followed her down the narrow corridors, through a set of thick steel doors guarded by a couple Procyon security men. I hadn't been through this section of the base. But it was new-ish, and I hadn't gotten the full tour. We wound up at the base of a stairwell and climbed until daylight brightened the railings on either side.

"I took the liberty of having our Chicago office send over one of their aircraft. You should find it the better version of a helicopter."

Loredana wasn't kidding. I'd expected to find another Blackhawk sitting outside the door at the top of the stairs, or maybe a civilian model. I stepped out into a broad clearing hemmed in by tall pines and surrounded by a rusty chain link fence. The vehicle at the center was unmistakable—same pale gray as any other military craft, except it was absent all markings. Nothing could identify it as belonging to Procyon.

Which was a good thing, because I was pretty sure the average community foundation wasn't supposed to have an Osprey tiltrotor, whether they fought monsters or not.

It sat there like its namesake, crouched on a building, ready to spring on its prey. Huge black propellers dangled from the end of long pylons.

Ramos donned his mirrored sunglasses and, to my surprise, smiled. "I won't bother placing my call, unless you need a trained pilot."

Loredana shielded her eyes. "I have one of those, as well, provided he's not killed himself in some foolish aerial maneuver."

A lanky guy with light brown hair spotted us and waved from an open hatch. He hopped down and trotted over.

"Looks like he hasn't died yet," I quipped.

"Not for lack of trying," Loredana murmured.

The pilot stopped short, pale cheeks flush. He cracked a grin. "Mighty fine day for a flight ain't it, Miss Lark?"

"Indeed it is. Though it appears it'll be nightfall by the time we get underway."

The pilot waved a hand. He had on an olive-drab flight suit over a garish, neon blue Hawaiian shirt patterned with green palm. "Don't bother me none. I reckon we'll put this bird through her paces, day or night."

"I'd like to introduce the operative leading this sortie, Mercury Hale."

"Pleasure to make your acquaintance." The guy wrung my hand like he'd never heard of a dryer for getting moisture out of laundry.

"Yeah, uh, the same. You're the new guy? From Chicago?"

He winked. "Thereabouts. Copernicus Sark, finest pilot this side of Galderica and anywhere else that's a blamed sight farther across the Interstice."

CHAPTER ELEVEN

So, we had a pilot, albeit one who smiled way too much. The crew was still in recovery.

Have to say, I wasn't a fan of the way Bowen limped as we headed for the infirmary. That didn't keep him from his goal, even when he had to stop to take a breath.

"Using those powers—it drains you, huh?" I leaned against the wall.

"Yes. But here more so than home." He wiped sweat from his brow. Some of the pink leeched back into his cheeks. Hand still shook, though. "I have fought other summoners of great power before. In the wake of those battles, there have been moments in which I felt I had perhaps taken one step too far. As if I were meant to finally plunge over the edge of an isle into the last drop to the sea."

Pieces of what he'd been saying started to connect. "Your islands... They fly?"

"Not all. Many. Hence the need for cloudships

with which to traverse the sky."

"So, what, you have blimps?"

His turn to blink.

"Hot air balloons."

"Ah. Nothing powered by fire, no. Aethershards buoy our vessels, the same crystals harvested from the floating isles themselves."

Wow. Okay. "If and when we get you back, I want a tour."

Bowen chuckled. "Your spirit impresses me, Mercury. I would be privileged to have you as one of my crew for a voyage, would but we could guarantee your safe return."

"Don't have to worry about that." I rapped on the prosthetic leg. "If I were obsessed with safety, this wouldn't have happened. Also, the world would have been destroyed two or three times, but hey, who's counting?"

We found Niall sitting up in his bed—or trying to, because Doc Arne kept pushing him down by pressing on his shoulder. "Intolerable!" Niall howled. "Bowen! By the clouds, it's about time you've come back. Tell this imbecile I'm fit to fight, not to be swaddled in blankets like a helpless babe."

"I do not think it wise to argue with this man of medicine." Bowen's tone was serious as any preacher's, but there was no disguising the smirk forming on his face. "Perhaps catching a metal cloudship injured you more than you care to admit."

"What—? I'm—There's nothing wrong with me!"

You don't get to see people splutter a lot, but man, Niall sure spluttered. He tried to sit up again, this time dodging around Doc Arne's outstretched hand. "Of all the addle-brained—!"

"Stay. In. Bed." Doc Arne slammed his palm flat against Niall's chest. "If you so much as put a finger over the side, I'll dose you with enough tranquilizers to put a herd of elephants to sleep, understand?"

Niall's eyes formed emerald slits. His lip curled back. Really hoped he wasn't planning a were-fox transformation in our cramped infirmary. "Captain..."

"At ease, Niall." Bowen pulled Doc Arne aside. "Surely, Doctor, he's not that bad off. I would venture that his attitude has suffered no undue harm."

Niall rolled his eyes. Doc Arne squinted. "He's stubborn, I'll agree, and his head must be made of something thicker than bone because he's managed not to crack his skull. Even with a helicopter landing on it."

"So, he's unhurt." I craned my neck for a look at Doc Arne's tablet.

"Un—No, he's not unhurt, Mercury. The man suffered internal hemorrhaging that is, thankfully, on the mend. But I'm not about to let him walk out of here—"

"Look, Doc. These debates are always a blast. This time, we're short of options. So, you're gonna have to let Niall walk out of here or I'm going to have Bowen freeze you to the floor and I'll carry him out myself."

Doc Arne's eyes went wide. Only the beeping of medical equipment interrupted the silence. Then Niall muttered, "As if the boy could lift me."

"Is this what Ms. Lark has to say?" Arne's monotone was kinda depressing, since I was used to high-powered rants.

"Didn't ask her." I folded my arms. "What's your call?"

Arne scowled until I thought his handlebar moustache was gonna poke him in the eyes. "If anything happens to him, I'm holding you responsible. I mean that, Mercury. I've had my fill of you and your superiors interfering in my medical care."

"I get that. If it were me, I'd be just as mad. But you know we're dealing with bodies that aren't all the way human, Doc. You've got to give us more leeway. The things we're facing... They're not going to hang around in the waiting room reading a magazine while your patients heal."

"Believe it or not, I've thought of that." He sighed and shook his head. Then he waved with his tablet. "Go on, get out. All of you."

Niall bounded from the bed. He immediately winced and held his side.

"Stitch from running?" Doc Arne quipped.

"Minor twinge." Niall grinned. "Far less painful than the wounds I'm yearning to inflict."

"Fine. Don't call me when your spleen falls out, because I don't have extras."

I sent Bowen and Niall off toward the armory, so they could retrieve their gear from Garvey. Me? I needed a quiet corner from which to make a phone call.

The number went to voicemail after five rings. "Hi, you've reached Dominic Zein. I'm away from my phone or otherwise indisposed—"

I rolled my eyes and redialed. Voicemail. I hung up and dialed again. And again. And—

"There's a reason I'm not answering your calls." Dominic Zein's voice had a smooth, mellow cadence to it, like he could have taken up a career as a Las Vegas lounge singer if the whole architect thing didn't work out. "And her name is Jess."

"When are you gonna introduce me to your wife, anyway, Gemini?" I raised my voice. "Sorry for the interruption!"

"Stop it." Dominic's voice lowered. "She's sleeping."

"Already?" I checked my watch. Late afternoon. "I though Colorado was an hour earlier than California."

"Mercury..."

"Did you even get my messages? The giant monster that's burning down the forest around San Camillo?"

"I did."

I waited for the part where he'd ask me for a location to which he could teleport, or when he should arrive by, or... something besides exhaling carbon dioxide into the receiver of his cell phone.

"And?"

"And what, Mercury? I'm not your rapid-transit system. I'm spending much-needed time with my wife. Ask Loredana. She's aware of my schedule."

"Your schedule? We're not talking about whether or not you've got time to present floor plans for a swanky convenience store."

"Don't forget that I'm considered on call for Procyon, and that I have my own mission with our organization."

"Sure. Evil twins."

"The doppelgangers from the other Earth pose a clear and present danger to our way of life. I've brought two more into custody since we ended the threat to San Camillo." Dominic blew out a breath. "If Loredana orders me, I'll show up. But I can't make any promises. Not when I'm monitoring the whereabouts of another infiltrator. What about Airfoil?"

"MIA."

"That's troubling. Does anyone at Procyon know his whereabouts?"

"He's not exactly on our payroll or showing up for company picnics." I rubbed my forehead. "Okay, look—I'll send you the coordinates Liz has. If there's any way you can drop in, even just to pin this sucker down..."

"As I said, I'll do my best. If Loredana has a new set of orders. Godspeed, Mercury."

"Great. Thanks."

So, that didn't go so great. It wasn't a "no," but it wasn't a "yes." Somehow, I doubted Loredana would order Dominic to drop everything and join the fight. Besides, how could I justify dragging him away from his wife? He was right—this was local trouble. I had plenty of backup.

"Feeling down?"

Wilhelmina must have been standing around the bend from where I'd had my conversation with Dominic. Either that or she'd added teleportation to her skill set. "Like I could burrow another hundred feet below this place. Eavesdrop much?"

"Only enough to hear you did fine handling things." She patted my cheek. "Been a pleasure watching you grow."

"Maturity's my new gig."

"Oh, I didn't say you'd made it all the way to adulthood, child. Headed in the right direction. And speaking of which—what's our word on the upcoming scenic flight?"

"Me and Bowen and Niall."

"Ain't forgetting me, now are you?"

"I wasn't about to speak for you." I smirked. "You know, in case you needed a nap."

She swatted at the top of my head with a knitting needle. "Mind your elders, Mercury, lest they have to whup you. Which you're fully aware I could do."

"Whatever you say." To be fair, I'd seen her fight. She'd handled enemies that wore me down, and when I was gone from this dimension to find Loredana and

Ramos, San Camillo had Wilhelmina as its protector. Not too shabby for someone three times my age and native to this dimension.

"So, what is it that ails you? Your frame's healing well enough. The soul's another matter."

"More like the heart. When are we gonna get a break from this? I mean, I've got a wedding coming up. How am I supposed to pretend that life's all normal—worrying about the caterer and the color of napkins—when there's another creature trying to burn everything down? This time, literally."

"Sounds like you're whining."

I chuckled. That was about the kind of pep talk I'd come to expect from her. "Maybe I am. I've saved the world a bunch. Aren't I entitled to some whining?"

"You're entitled to be human."

"Which I'm not."

She made with her hand like she was gonna smack me again, but I playfully blocked the incoming blow. "You got to stop thinking like that! The folks of Meda, those warriors like your parents who ventured over to our side centuries past, they were and are as human as the next man down the street. They've been granted a terrible responsibility—guardianship over weapons unmatched by anything we know of. Some of us are blessed enough to share in that heritage, to help lift the burden from time to time. But we've all got to lift, you know. Ain't much time for the mundane."

"I figured. Just needed to say it out loud."

"And you wouldn't be a normal man if you didn't." She smiled. "'Cause the end of that road's a long ways off. Thankfully, there's not a one of us who's got to walk it alone."

"Also figured. Which means, I take it, that you're coming on this crazy plane ride."

"It'll be a walk in the park, child. 'Sides—you're not the one driving."

The sky was bleeding into dusk by the time Liz got a good fix on the astral fury. Its track on the main monitor had curved away from San Camillo, but it reappeared in a streak of burning forest arcing back toward the city.

"If I didn't know any better," I said, "It's trying to surround us."

"A disturbing thought." Loredana had changed into her other set of work clothes—gray T-shirt, slate colored military-style pants, boots, and a ballcap. She fitted a Kevlar vest across her chest. "Do we have assurance that fire crews are clear of the area?"

"They're too busy keeping the flames from advancing on populated areas," Ramos said. "You won't have anyone stumbling into the crossfire—and all the smoke ought to conceal your activities."

"A pity." Niall slung the SCAR over his shoulder. He rested a hand on the pommel of his sword. "It will be a grand fight for your magic glass to show the masses."

"And a fair sight more entertaining than you wrestling with an Ursanite," Bowen said.

"I won that match, I'll remind you. Gave the silver to the orphans…"

"Sakes, boys." Wilhelmina whacked Bowen in the ribs with her knitting bag. "If I'd known y'all yap as much as Mercury, I'd have gone to the Y for the cribbage tournament. Now, we going to vanquish this critter or stand around chatting all night?"

Bowen and Niall stared at her. They looked like guys trying to find just the right verbal comeback but unsure how to wield it against an old lady. I saved them further embarrassment. "Let's load up, boys and girls. Our winged steed awaits."

The Osprey's rotors were churning the air, kicking dust and pine needles into a frenzy. Tiny green lights on the end of each one turned the spinning blades into phosphorescent rings. Red and white lights blinked on the wingtips and fuselage.

"How's she fare, Cope?" Loredana shouted over the prop wash as we strode up the ramp at the back of the aircraft.

"Right and rarin' to fly, Miss Lark!" Cope had on his own baseball cap, bearing the Chicago Cubs logo. He took a bag from her and stowed it inside netting. I kept the huge ice gun nearby, lodged between the bench and the wall behind me. There was plenty of netting to anchor it. "Mind your heads and find a chair!"

We strapped into the jump seats as he closed the

hatch. I gave Loredana's hand a quick squeeze. "I thought about arguing for you to stay behind, but I figured that was a lost cause."

"That's correct." She kissed me on the cheek. "I can think of no better way for us to keep each other safe than to watch each other's backs."

"Well, that, or stay home altogether." I grinned.

"And we both know that's not an option."

"Ladies and gentlemen!" Cope's voice filtered back from the cockpit. "Welcome aboard the non-stop flight from your favorite hidden bunker into the burning depths of Avernus itself! I'd advise hangin' on to something, as I'll do my blamed best to find us turbulence. Enjoy!"

The Osprey lurched skyward and before I knew it, I could see the darkened airfield with the small bunker entrance outside the portholes. We must have been flying nearly perpendicular.

"Mercury!" Bowen held onto his straps, but there was a looseness to his grip. He was alert, but if he was scared, he wasn't showing it. Wilhelmina was nestled between him and Niall. "This land is full of noise!"

"You just now noticed?" I shouted back. "We're not big on tranquil settings at Procyon!"

"It is your world itself! The machines are wondrous and terrifying, but they clamor with constant need for attention. A cloudship whispers to its captain, sometimes in soft reminder, other times in urgent rejoinder. We rise to the winds and they take us where they will. Here, you go where you want with incredible speed, yet the journey is lost."

I could see his point, but I wasn't in the mood to get philosophical. "Tell you what—hold on to your buckles and leave the flying for the guy who knows his noise."

"Noise? Branterspit!" Cope whooped from the cockpit. "This here's the contented purr of a sabertooth full up from her favorite meal! I wouldn't trade the racket for an empty tomb!"

I leaned in closer to Loredana. "Where in Chicago did you say you dug him up?"

"I did not dig him up anywhere, nor did he originate from Chicago."

"Not Meda or the alternate Earth, either, I'm guessing."

"None of those or this world, and none to which you've yet visited." Loredana kept her gaze firmly on the opposite bulkhead. "Let us say, he fell into our laps. Ask him about biplanes, when you have a chance."

Right. We bounced through turbulent air so hard my feet came up off the deck. Wilhelmina yelped and made the sign of the cross. Bowen touched her shoulder, but he was smiling. Niall flat out beamed.

Just me and my fiancée, on our flight courtesy of a crazy pilot to go fight an interdimensionally-combined flame monster, dragging a senior citizen and two *Final Fantasy* extras into battle.

CHAPTER TWELVE

We flew northeast, the Osprey bouncing along like we were on a state road in need of major maintenance after said state's major budget cuts. Seriously, could you have potholes in the air? I'm not bad with flying but the last trip through the air I took was on Loredana's custom private jet. That was as smooth as sliding into bed.

"Hey!" I propped myself inside the cockpit door. "You want to keep it on the road up there?"

"Friend, you'd best keep your rear end back in this bird's rear end, snug and strapped in." Cope had both hands on the controls, the muscles in his arms taut like steel cables but his voice as friendly as if we were sharing a beer on the bayside Promenade. "I don't cotton to mouthy passengers. And I reckon you don't want your skull bouncing off the ceiling when we hit the big bumps."

"The big bumps." The plane jerked suddenly to the left. My shoulder rebounded off the hatch frame.

"Like these aren't big enough?"

"It's only going to get worse before it gets better. All that there hot air blowing off that fella—thermal updrafts would be great to lift a teratorn looking to soar, but they play havoc with a bird like this."

He didn't have to point out "that fella." I could see the astral fury good enough. It was the writhing blob of flame undulating over the distant hills. Those fiery tendrils lashed every which way, setting trees alight—not that there were many left that hadn't been charred to a cinder. The air filled with sparks. Smoke clouds caught the ruddy glow from the blaze, giving what should have been a lovely place to hike a hellish appearance.

"Don't worry about the bumps, I guess." My stomach twisted. It had nothing to do with the turbulence. "Just get us in close enough we can engage the astral fury."

"Won't be able to linger airborne, nearer we get," Cope said. "I'm not keen on testing heat tolerances."

"Yeah, well, I want a Maserati but we're both going to be disappointed, right?" I reached out and slapped his shoulder. "Good job not getting us killed so far."

Cope chuckled. "High praise, indeed! Let the lady know we're a few miles out."

A few miles. Great.

I staggered back to the cargo bay, where everyone else was seated. Except for Bowen and Niall, who were peering out the portholes. How were they not toppling over like drunken frat boys? "Got a few more miles until we can hit the thing!"

"Good!" Niall gestured with his rifle. "Through this hatch?"

"That's the plan!" A terrifying plan, but *the* plan, at the moment. Subject to change without warning. "I need you guys to pin it down so I can use the ice gun to do the real damage—with a certain wizard as backup!"

"Summoner," Bowen said. "And I look forward to ending the beast's depredations with our combined might."

"You and me both."

Wilhelmina had her eyes closed. I touched her knee. Big mistake. A knitting needle sliced through the air. I jerked my hand back, so the needle stabbed between two fingers and poked into the worn-out seat cushion. "Don't sneak up on a body like that!"

"Easy! I'm checking to make sure you're okay."

"Do I look 'okay,' child? I may never eat again."

"That's too bad, because I could eat an entire pie from Carlito's. I'd be willing to share."

One eye cracked open. Stormy blue glared at me. The needle hovered surprisingly still in the tumult of the cargo by. "Say it again, Mercury, and the astral fury won't be but a pleasant dream."

"How nice to see morale is unaffected." Loredana didn't seem afraid, but she didn't appear well, either. Her face was a couple shades paler than usual. Freckles stood out like measles. "I suggest you gentlemen work on acquiring a target."

"Two miles!" Cope yelled.

"Let's do this." I reached past Bowen and slapped a switch mounted on the airframe.

The entire bay flooded with red light. An alarm buzzed. The rear door cracked open. Air rushed in—hot air, fresh out of a hairdryer. Sparks and soot swirled around.

"Oh, he's seen us! I don't think he's happy about it." Cope laughed. "Chin up, fellows, I'll bank on the port wing and bring us around."

Bank he did, though how the incline was so gentle I had no clue, not with all the bouncing around the Osprey insisted on maintaining. I retrieved the ice gun and propped it against the frame. Thankfully Liz had rigged up a set of straps that hooked onto the ballistic vest I wore.

Bowen stood four steps away from me, on the hinge where the hatch lowered. The wind blasted at his hair and his clothes. Even without the cape, he looked every bit the majestic sky captain, hands on his hips. A faint blue glow seeped from between his fingers.

"You ready for this?" I shouted as energies poured into the ice gun from the pulsar stave.

He turned. It was a really good thing I'd made a pit stop before we'd departed, because I wasn't sure how my bladder would have responded to the sight of his piercing, glowing eyes in that blood red environment. Think Superman about to unleash his heat vision, except the light was the coldest, most brilliant white tinged with blue. "I am prepared."

No backing out.

And there it was.

The astral fury must have had another growth spurt since thrashing downtown San Camillo. I guessed he was a couple hundred feet across, based on the size of the trees beneath him.

"My word," was all Loredana had.

"Light him up!" I pulled the trigger.

The ice gun bucked in my grip. A spiral of energy slashed through the red night sky, slamming into one pulsating, bulbous side of the giant jellyfish. Steam exploded. Blue blots skittered across its flanks.

"*Glacii*!" Bowen shouted the word like it was the last sound he was gonna let loose from his lungs. Twin sprays of jagged ice hurtled from his palms. I was super glad it was the astral fury and not me in the crosshairs of Bowen's hands as those two-foot shards cut through its hide—and I do mean, through. Several blasted apart burning trees on the other side of the monster.

And it was—displeased. I swore its scream shook the Osprey as Cope kept us in a sharp loop around the burned-out clearing.

"Pin it down!" I didn't know what other commands to issue because, you know, it was my first time using the pulsar stave adapted to a gun that mimicked ice powers. I just let the weapon blast away, the exterior getting colder with each passing second.

Feeling the frigid pulsar stave in my hands was one thing. This? I was sure Doc Arne was gonna have to cut off some frostbitten fingers while he repeated, "I told you so."

Suddenly a column of fire shot into the sky, no more than a car's length from the Osprey's tail. The heat bowled us over. Bowen tottered on the edge of the ramp, his boots slipping.

Niall snagged him one-handed, while looping his other arm through stray webbing. "Hold fast!"

"I'd rather you did!" Bowen redirected his palms, showering the column in ice.

It would have dampened the new element pretty well, except another tower shot forth—and then a third.

"Great," I muttered.

"If I didn't know better, I'd say our little critter down there's found a new trick to show off!" Wilhelmina cried out.

"You think?" I glanced at Loredana. "See how Cope's doing!"

"Cope's been taking a gander at the skies ahead, and they ain't the welcoming kind!" Cope hollered.

The Osprey slewed sideways and dropped like a rock. I yelped and grabbed for Loredana—not to stop myself from hitting the wall, but to haul her back from the hatch. Everything in the aircraft reversed direction. I couldn't tell which way we were headed.

All I knew was the flames shooting by the windows were way too close.

"Strap in!" Cope ordered. "Tarnation! You all need to hold on tight while I do my blamedest to get make sure we don't scorch our feathers!"

Loredana held on to my shoulder as we edged to the cockpit. The engines roared through the metal fuselage. Cope was twisted in his seat, shoulder up, fighting to maintain control. The ground outside, the treetops and the burning grass, were getting nearer.

"Find us a landing zone," Loredana said. "We'll set down there and approach the target on foot."

"Miss Lark, I'll be frank, there's not a time I'd disrespect a woman, but I'll make an exception if you don't secure yourself!" he snapped. "Sit down and hold on!"

Cope threw the Osprey sideways, flipping up in the opposite direction. I slammed against the cockpit wall. Loredana landed on me, which was better for her. I got a fire extinguisher jammed against my spine as a reward.

But I couldn't blame Cope for new bruises. His sudden aerobatics had put distance between us and the nearest tower of fire. Another one shot up a few dozen feet from the nose. We were gonna fly right through it and I didn't want to guess whether or not the Osprey's fuselage would like taking a flame shower at hundreds of degrees.

Cope muttered and cranked the controls. The plane shuddered and jumped, lifting, racing the pinnacle of the rising column of flames. For a moment, I imagined I could feel heat underfoot—and could smell melting metal. Then we were through it, back into reddish sky.

"There." Loredana pointed.

All I could see was a black smudge amidst trees backlit with crimson. Landing zone? Looked more like a postage stamp.

"Sharp eyes," Cope said. "Now if you folks don't mind, I'd best put this bird down with as minimal fuss as possible."

He wove the Osprey through more fire columns that sprouted from the ground. How he could see through the thick smoke and past the spray of embers, I had no idea. All I knew was Cope didn't let himself be distracted by the bang of objects against the fuselage, or warning lights flashing on his console, or shouts from the back of the plane. The Osprey banked left, dodged right, all while dropping nearer to the treetops.

Then we were among them.

The fires had burned a jagged gash through the forest, courtesy of the astral fury's trek. It made for a great space in which Cope could hide the aircraft from the monster's attacks; sure enough, as soon as we dipped below the treeline, the fire columns ceased.

Of course, it didn't hide the fact that we were flying through the forest instead of over it.

"One minute!" Cope reached up and snapped a trio of switches above his head. "Gather your crew and prepare to bail!"

"Bail?" I gave his seat a shove. "You said we were

headed for a landing zone!"

"Reckon so! And land we will—for about fifteen seconds, on ten feet of air! Now move!"

Even Loredana didn't argue with the order. She was already in the cargo bay, shouting commands and strapping on a backpack.

"Everybody up!" I helped Wilhelmina out of her restraints. The bemused part of me wondered if AARP was gonna have my head on a platter for endangering one of their members. I told the bemused part to shut up.

"Are we near to docking this vessel?" Niall asked.

"More like leaping overboard." I checked the ice gun. The bindings were secure, and I had a good grip on it. Made a mental note to not land on the thing when we jumped.

I fully expected Niall's complaints and sarcasm, but instead got a shout of joy. "And here I thought this land was only for the faint-of heart!"

"Seriously?" I shook my head. "I did tackle the monster three times already."

"I'm putting her down and everybody had better get out!" Cope yelled.

Trees whipped past the open hatch. Suddenly, the Osprey spun around, and slammed to a halt so fast I almost wound up flat on my face. It bobbed, the wind buffeting its sides, the rotors' roar whining to a crescendo.

"Boots away!" Niall was the first one off.

Bowen just shook his head and dove after.

Wilhelmina examined the edge of the bouncing ramp. I stood beside her. "Are you sure you're—?"

"Yep!" She vanished over the edge.

Well okay then.

Loredana took my hand. "Together?"

"Absolutely." I turned around and gave a sloppy, fake salute. "All yours!"

"Good luck and Thel keep you!" Cope pulled back on the controls.

The ramp and the whole plane tilted precipitously. I let myself slide, then jumped, Loredana alongside.

We hit open air. It was like diving into a dryer, minus the lint trap, but plus scalding embers and suffocating smoke. The ground and I were gonna get acquainted really soon. I twisted, trying to ready my legs for impact.

Blue light suffused everything. My rear end hit a smooth, cold surface, and I slid faster than I had down any playground slide. That includes those slick metal ones that are now considered safety hazards.

Loredana and I tumbled into a crispy shrub. It crumbled under our impact. Bonus: We were covered with enough soot we could have tried out for the Mary Poppins movie sequel, if we could dance as well as chimney sweeps.

I glanced back. A chute of ice was already melting in the intense heat. Had to be twice as long as the Osprey.

Bowen shook his right hand, as if he were trying to get feeling back into his digits. "What good would it do us to leap into battle only to be killed in the fall?"

"Wise guy and handy to have around." I helped Loredana up.

The Osprey shot straight up from the clearing, pivoted its rotors, and shot away from the forest. Sounded an awful lot like someone cheering as it roared away, strands of fire leaping in its wake.

"I suppose I shall have to add a supplemental line for hazard pay in our next budget," Loredana murmured.

"Only if you want to hire a replacement when he gets himself blown up." I didn't feel any broken bones. Loredana looked good—duh, I meant in the injury sense—and Bowen was busy checking his unsheathed sword for damage. "Everybody else okay?"

"Nary a bruise," Wilhelmina said. "I couldn't have prayed for a softer landing."

Probably because she was only now disembarking from Niall's burly arms. She seemed to be taking her sweet time. As soon as her shoes touched dirt, she got on tiptoe and grabbed Niall's chin. She planted a great big smooch on his cheek.

Niall's face went red as his hair, an impressive feat, given that everything in the clearing was colored a flickering orange from the flames.

"Devotees abound." Bowen chuckled and shook his head. "Onward, then?"

I was gonna give a great speech about the need to

stick together, watch each other's backs, and even give Bowen and Wilhelmina a chance to pray for us—if they were so inclined—when the air in the center of the clearing whipped up into a dust devil. A person-sized one. White light exploded from a pinprick, expanding into a translucent globe with a black void at its middle.

By the time we all took cover, the light and wind abated. A man stood in its place, clad in an all-black outfit, including fingerless gloves with rubber-reinforced knuckles. The tall collar of his compression shirt added to the mysterious, special agenty look, topped off by a mask that covered his face from the bridge of his nose down. Deep brown eyes widened.

"Ah," Loredana said. "Very good."

Dominic pulled down the mask and squinted through the smoke. "You all look awful. Am I too late for the battle?"

"Seriously?" I threw my arms wide open. Bowen had to duck, because otherwise I would have taken his head off with the ice gun. "That maniac pilot nearly killed us, and you could've—Argh! It would've been so easy to—! Just beamed us in without—!"

"Mercury." Loredana put both hands on my shoulders. She locked her gaze with mine. "Let's not dwell on that. We have the mission."

I blew out a breath. "Okay fine." I swiped soot from her face. She could have been reading for a football game—or rugby, or whatever. "But after this, we go somewhere cool and wet. No heat. No fires.

A chilly cruise."

She smiled. "I shall hold you to your promise, after we kill our prey."

What a romantic she was.

CHAPTER THIRTEEN

The only thing more surreal than leading my mangy pack of fighters through the burning thicket toward the giant monster looming overhead was my phone ringing in the middle of us striding forth.

I totally forgot I'd brought it. The earbud spent so much time in, well, my ear that I got used to its presence. "This had better not be a sales call, and yes, I'm happy with my car insurance."

A familiar giggle broke through. "Do you get those on your cell, too? I thought it was just me! I mean I know it's worse if you have a landline and I keep telling Lieutenant Ramos he should just get rid of it as soon as all his kids have phones but did you know he's not going to let them have their own until—"

"Liz. Updates?" A hissing sound rose. Bowen shot ice toward the biggest blazes, doing his best to douse them.

"Oh. Sure. Yeah, our readings are off the charts."

"Sounds like you need bigger charts."

"That's not a bad idea, actually. I'll bet I could have Cyril extend the maximum—"

"Liz!" I could see the swaying tentacles from the astral fury framed between blackened tree trunks, only a few hundred yards ahead. Hadn't spotted us yet, but I wasn't waiting until it did. "The monster!"

"Yeah, I know! He's huge! Tachyon emissions are near overwhelming the sensors. I had to pull the drones clear back to the 311 or they were gonna get fried. Even there, it's taxing their hardware. I bet I could step outside the bunker and get readings as clear. So, the problem is, the dimensional fabric is warping?"

Bowen and Niall hunkered low, fanning out on either side of us, as we approached the huge burned-out home of the astral fury. Niall carried his gun like he'd been born in Special Forces, while Bowen slunk along with his sword gleaming in the orange light of this hundred-acre campfire. Loredana nudged me and gestured with her weapon of choice, the MP5.

"Okay. Dimensional fabric warping is bad, right?"

"Yeah, pretty bad. It means the place where Bowen and Niall came from is bleeding into our dimension and vice versa. I mean, portals are one thing Mercury, and a more permanent bridge like the Transect that Gemini uses to get to the alternate Earth is another, but it's a bad idea for dimensions to touch. Never mind that the astral fury could go back and start attacking people over there. The warping can make both dimensions—hiccup."

"Hiccup. Care to explain?"

"Sorry. Can't. I could have Cyril run scenarios for you, but the amount of data means you'd need to get yourself a Ph.D. in the next half hour, so…" She slurped on the dregs of a soda. I heard plastic clatter against a concrete floor. "The summary? Imagine a pair of bubbles bumping into each other. They sometimes pop."

"Okay. Cool. Earth could pop."

That got all five pairs of eyes trained on me. Dominic mouthed, "Pop?"

I blew out my breath. "So, got any advice besides put our heads between our legs and kiss our butts goodbye?"

"We slay the beast!" Niall snarled.

"Yeah, yeah, I remember, Braveheart. Liz?"

"No, he's right. I've had Narang cutting apart the tendril—maybe pieces of it, not the whole thing. The hide's not all that different from a regular astral fiend, only it has the fire-producing capacity and acts as a massive insulating system. Keeps the fury from burning its own insides, plus it stockpiles tachyon particles in a way the astral fiends could only dream of. If you can cut through and deliver a killing blow with the pulsar stave's directed energy—"

"We can melt him. Like the rest."

"Yeah! Exactly. I mean, the problem is keeping

him cold long enough to do it."

"Oh, don't worry about that." I patted the gun. "We've got the tools. Now I just need the plan. Thanks for that."

"You're welcome! Stay safe. Um… Is Niall okay?"

I blew Niall a kiss and winked at him. He looked ready to cut my head off. Totally worth it. "Liz says 'Hi,' big dog."

Liz giggled again. "You're terrible. 'Bye!'"

Loredana was shaking her head. "You really are, you know."

"You still love me." I grinned. "Okay, gang, let's do this."

"What is 'this' that we're planning to do?" Bowen straightened. I got the feeling I'd ruined whatever tactics he and Niall had worked out. "Since we are evidently abandoning the hunter's approach."

"Here's the deal—I've got to be the one to put the stab into the astral fury. I need two people to distract it, while Bowen and I ice it down. Dominic's our transport—he'll zip us around the fury so we can keep it off balance."

"Can you keep a giant floating monster off balance, technically speaking?" Dominic was staring up through the trees at it.

Was it getting bigger?

"Mercury!" That stewas Liz again. "The breach between dimensions is growing! I'm getting a spike of—out of reach with—there's—"

Her signal cut out. And we could all see why. A

granddaddy of all rips opened high above the astral fury, a great squirming slash of purple light. I could see more sky beyond it. A weird pattern of stars, a peaceful velvety night with a handful of tranquil clouds scudding by.

"I never dreamed I would be terrified of seeing the way home," Bowen murmured. "We must end this."

"And send you back." I primed the ice gun... then withdrew the pulsar stave. I separated its halves. "Here."

I held one out to Dominic. He held up his hands. I could see the silvery glint from the Echo Watches around his wrists, just beneath his shirt cuffs. "Don't you need that for the gun?"

"Nope. You get it. Because of those things." I tapped on his sleeve. Metal rang out. "They're from Meda, right? You carry the same kind of genetic marker Wilhelmina does, then—a human from Earth with the capability of using Medan tech. So, use it."

Dominic's fingers curled around the stave. It pulsed with energy. Not the same brilliant flare I could summon, but once he plugged it into the gun, the weapon powered up. "I—didn't think that was possible. But why not Wilhelmina? We barely know each other."

"Doesn't matter none." Wilhelmina extended the Medan-forged dagger from her knitting bag. The tachyon modifier attached to the hilt hummed, emitting a familiar yellow-white hue. "This little blade can strengthen me, child, but I won't be hefting that refrigerator around on these old legs. You go on now. I'll manage."

By manage, she meant leaping straight up to the treetops.

Niall laughed uproariously. "Do not leave but a ruined corpse for me to carve!" He morphed into his fox-man form and did some serious parkour up the trunks to join her, the two of them bounding through branches toward the astral fury's tentacles.

"Or, I don't know, we could just dump the plan and randomly charge." I sighed and shook my head.

"Everybody present your bus passes." Dominic held out his wrists.

The rest of us circled up. Before Dominic could activate the Echo Watches, I realized what was missing. Same thing that had been absent from all these monster brawls lately. Tunes.

I tapped into my playlist and set it on shuffle. I needed something with a fast beat. Something edgy. What I got? Huey Lewis and the News belting "The Power of Love."

Oh, well. I glanced at Loredana. It'd get my heart going, one way or another.

Dominic formed the shimmering bubble, and, after we floated in what felt like zero gravity for a few second, the world blurred around us.

I caught a brief glimpse of a gorgeous, darkened forest. Crickets chirped beyond the rush of the portal's wind.

Then I bounced back into an inferno.

Great news! Didn't barf that time. I was falling from fifty feet above the astral fury, toward a bare patch surrounded by fire.

A stream of glowing ice hammered at the upper left flank of the fury, invoking a scream that had to have been heard on the moon. Bowen was chilling—see what I did there?—on a rocky outcropping. His eyes were blazing beacons of blue-white light, his left hand invisible behind a corona of the same ice-generating power. He used his left to swipe the spiny end of a tentacle that got to close to him, coating the falchion blade in dripping ichor.

I landed atop the fiend and struggled for footing on the pliable hide. The prosthetic leg spazzed. A couple more seconds and I wouldn't have survived the attack. Tendrils sprayed flame as they slapped at me. I whirled the pulsar stave, slicing them apart. Liz wasn't kidding. The fury wasn't concerned with inflicting damage on itself because no matter how razor sharp or fiery hot those tendrils looked, they weren't even singeing the hide.

A howl echoed across the clearing. Niall hurtled through a sheet of flame, red and white fur and fangs and claws. One paw brandished the katana. The other? Firing with the SCAR rifle. How in the world did he fit his finger around the trigger? Maybe that's what the claw was for.

Bullets cut through the outer layer of the hide, ripping a gap along the opposite flank. Tendrils pivoted and went for the intercept.

A new beam of light hit the fury underneath, slicing upward into its—belly? Who knew? A black silhouette stood among fallen trees. The moment the monster's tentacles went thrashing in his direction, Dominic vanished in a blink of light. The astral fury pounded empty ground.

Another cry broke through the cacophony. That was Wilhelmina. She came flying from a stand of trees, their tops swaying from her departure, in a somersault that I'd be hard pressed to duplicate. She slit a tentacle down the middle using her dagger, then lopped it off at the base when she landed thirty feet away.

"Start digging!" My voice was hoarse. I needed a drink. Heck, I could have sucked on an iceberg.

More gunfire erupted. Loredana was perched halfway up a tall pine, raking another side of the astral fury with bullets. Dominic was beside her, lending the ice gun's brilliant beam to the mix.

A tentacle snapped out, quick as a lightning strike, and broke their branch.

I sliced off two more tendrils and started to run for them, but Dominic caught Loredana around the waist and they blinked out of existence.

Niall roared. A tendril wrapped around his bicep, but he pulled so hard he ripped it clean off, then slashed another with the katana. He rolled under a spray of fire and emptied half the rifle's magazine into the hide at his feet, until he was standing in a rippling pool of blue slime and black flesh.

"We're through!" I shouted. No idea if anyone but Wilhelmina and Niall could hear me.

Loredana and Dominic burst from a flare of light, right next to me. Okay, that was slick.

I pointed down.

Loredana nodded. She ejected the magazine from her gun and loaded a new one. "Very good. Mr. Phelan, if you would?"

He slung the gun over his shoulder and sneered. "This will be vile."

I charged the pulsar stave, letting it build power. Wilhelmina was busy deflecting incoming tendrils. Dominic lent the Echo Watches to our defense, slinging blasts of golden energy that set the monster steaming—and doused a few fires, too.

Where was Bowen, anyway? I looked around at the trees—

Hang on. Where were the trees?

A breeze brushed my face. Cool breeze. The sky was a lot darker, too, and that purple rift in the sky was a lot bigger.

Or closer.

"Ah, guys?" I pointed up. "This thing's headed for the exit."

"Then perhaps it'd be best if you kill it!" Niall snapped.

He dug his claws into either side of the astral fury's gaping wound, and with a roar that shook my innards, tore it apart. He sank deeper into the muck, and the screams from the fury—let's just say they weren't leaving my head any time soon.

I dove into the wound. Bad idea. It was way hot in there. My head spun. Even the pulsar stave—half of it, anyway—wasn't enough to keep me cool. Liz could have measured the exact temperature to within a half degree. My vision swirled. I slashed as deep as I could with the stave, but the dumb creature refused to obliterate.

"Wrest him free!" a voice ordered from far above.

A furry set of claws dragged me up and out. The only thing that kept me from dying, I'm pretty sure, was the supersuit. Its haphazard patterns glowed bright enough I could have swum under San Camillo Bay from one side to the other at midnight. I could feel the energy it absorbed from the pulsar stave seeping back into my body.

"That's—ow. Not enough." I gasped. My chest ached.

"We know. Captain Cord has a solution." Loredana slid me away from the wound.

Bowen was high above us, standing atop a tower of ice that projected from the astral fury. Whether he'd pierced the thing or built it around, I had no clue, but the blue light from his eyes almost obliterated his face. Ice poured down, knifing into the wound. The crackling drowned out all other sounds except the astral fury's caterwauling.

"Here." Dominic took the pulsar stave from me and attached the half to its companion that was plugged into the ice gun. "You're up."

I staggered upright, swaying. Dominic caught my shoulder. Loredana was already propping me. Wilhelmina cried out. Niall leapt to her aid, joining the defense against the fury's onslaught. "Make it quick!" she shouted.

I held onto the ice gun until I thought it was going to rip my arms off, then pulled the trigger.

A second, more brilliant, more focused beam of ice joined Bowen's storm. The wound widened. Hide shriveled and pulled back. The combined ice shards and beams dug deeper, until there was a tunnel—a well—five feet across with glistening walls of frozen flesh reaching three or four times my height into the core of the astral fury.

Way down there, it pulsed pale blue like a summer morning's sky, swirls of purple chasing each other across slick innards.

Bingo.

But we were way too close to the rip between dimensions. Loredana shouted a warning. I craned my neck. There was an island, upside down. Vertigo threatened to knock me off my feet. Were we rising through my sky, or falling through Bowen's?

Huey Lewis made way for the Foo Fighters. Much better for the finale, I thought.

I yanked the pulsar stave from the ice gun, willed it to full strength until it made my eyes water, and dove headfirst into the well of flesh. Felt like I fell forever. Waves of heat rolled over me while spikes of cold dug through my chest. Breathing became a chore. I was ready to give it up.

The leg quit on me. Nothing but a dead hunk of plastic and titanium.

I wasn't dead yet. No way. I willed energy from the pulsar stave, redirected it through the suit, and channeled enough into the leg to return a semblance of feeling to it. Had to remind it who was in charge. Not just for me, but for Loredana, for Wilhelmina, Dominic and Bowen and Niall, Ramos and Liz, Garvey, heck, even Doc Arne—everyone who my feverish brain worried about as possible casualties. Don't even get started about the people in the city I called home. It was more overwhelming than the fluctuating temperatures and smothering stench.

Let me get rid of this guy. Please?

Whatever Ramos was doing then, I knew his version of the same plea would carry more weight.

The pulsar stave struck home.

Blackness engulfed me. A supernova of riotous colors displaced it. I spun around, clutching to the pulsar stave like it was both anchor and parachute. The familiar tug of dimensional travel disassembled my body and put it back together, a few more times than I could count. Really hoped none of that was the same as dying.

The whirlwind subsided. I landed in blue ooze, a thick sludge streaked with black. I spat grit from between my teeth. Sand?

It was a calm night. Cool, not too dark, because the velvet blue sky was replete with stars—more lights than I could imagine. Waves crashed nearby.

From forest fire to vacation beach.

The astral fury's form was like an oil slick, but one that was rapidly sublimating. I tried not to gag. Imagine the biggest landfill full of the ripest garbage, baking under 100-degree sun in humidity so thick you could doggie paddle the air.

"Mercury!" Dominic dropped to his knees. His outfit was more blue than black, thanks to the slime. He grinned great big. "Thank God. You did it!"

"We did." I coughed. Ow. Best to let the old tachyon-infused body heal before I hacked up a lung or some other equally important organ. "Loredana?"

"Here." She limped, her arm draped over Wilhelmina's shoulders. "My ankle is sprained, I believe."

I got up and hugged her. A good move, because she melted into my arms. And also, it kept me from passing out. Less than heroic.

"By the heavens." Bowen knelt on the sand. His sword was resting on his knee. "The Most High has brought us home and granted us victory."

"Amen," Dominic said.

"And what a victory!" Niall whooped. He drove the katana into the beach, where it stuck, quivering. "I know not what ails the rest of you but if I cannot find a tankard of mead on this isle, I demand we depart!"

"Yeah, well, mead apart, I've got a better idea." Loredana and I kissed. "Let's go home."

CHAPTER FOURTEEN

Maybe not home quite yet.

"You did promise me a cruise," Loredana said.

Wasn't gonna argue that.

So, we stood at the railing of Bowen's cloudship, the *Northwind*. I'd been on schooners out beyond San Camillo's breakers—felt the deck rolling with the waves, smelled the salt air, tasted the spray. This was like that but minus the spray, and a much smoother ride, because *Northwind* flew, probably two or three hundred feet above the starlit seas.

Bowen never looked more at home. No wonder I thought Skipper had been a crusty old sea captain. Seeing him in his element, turning the twin wheels to control our direction and height, with that ridiculous cloak billowing behind him, made me about as happy as being with Loredana did.

"A few days 'til home," he said. "I would be honored to have you both as guests."

I checked my watch. "As much fun as it'd be to hang out on angel island—"

"They're Aevorn," Niall said. "And you'd best recall their proper name, welp!"

"Yeah. Anyway, Dominic should be back any minute and then we've got to see if those fires have been knocked down."

"I would check with Elizabeth. Perhaps the ice gun can be put to a more peaceful use," Loredana said.

"You want to call her now?" I waved my phone.

Loredana pushed it away and smirked. "I doubt very much our service provider will allow communications over such a distance as this, and I'll not be the one to spoil the moment, thank you very much."

Nope, leave that duty to Dominic. His portal expanded halfway down the deck, between us and Bowen at the wheels. Wilhelmina was so busy following Niall's hand tracing a course across an unfurled chart that he had to pull her away from the swirling light.

When it cleared, two people stood on the deck—Dominic, still dressed in black but sans his mask, and a pretty woman of Middle Eastern heritage with flowing raven-hued hair.

"I don't believe it!" She clung to Dominic and sighed. "It's so lovely up here! The ship's really flying?"

"It is." Dominic caught me staring and winked.

"Since you interrupted my date, Mercury, I thought it only fair I return the gesture."

I chuckled. "Hey, you're not on my clock, Gemini, and since you're our ticket back to Earth, I don't think Loredana's going to complain, either."

She put her finger to my lips. "Less babble, more contemplation."

"Yes, ma'am."

The woman extended her hand. "Jessica Zein."

"Mercury Hale." I gestured to Loredana. "And she's—"

"Nice to see you again, Loredana." Jessica wrinkled her nose. "But you've smelled better."

"Haven't we all."

"Let's leave these two some privacy, Jess," Dominic said. "We've all earned it."

He was right. It was nice to step away from battle, and even from the ruckus that was life on good old real Earth. Plus, I finally got why Dominic was so tetchy about being forced to come to our aid. His life was his. He valued the same things I did—especially the things that mattered to his heart.

Probably I could cut him a break, then.

"You ready to go?" I asked Loredana. My leg ached. Wasn't going to give up standing any time soon, though.

"No. But I suppose we must, soon."

I nodded. "This isn't a paradise. Bowen and Niall—they came to our world primed to fight. Guns, swords, lethal magic... You don't need those if everything's perfect and beautiful."

"I agree, it's likely not a paradise."

"Nope. Probably has more monsters."

"Indeed."

"Means this break won't last us long. Even when we get back, there's the real world and the Interstice to deal with. That's our job. Our duty."

"I'm proud of you for taking both on. We will have to return, and when we do, I know you'll keep us in the fight."

"And you'll keep me grounded."

She smiled.

"But," I added, "Five more minutes won't kill us."

Mercury's adventures continue...

Stay tuned

www.steverzasa.com

www.ingramcontent.com/pod-product-compliance
Lightning Source LLC
Chambersburg PA
CBHW061216210726
48294CB00006B/1855